I0630238

MESSAGES FROM BEN

Ellen Parry Lewis

Metal Lunchbox Publishing

Copyright © 2025 Metal Lunchbox Publishing

All rights reserved

The characters and events portrayed in this book are fictitious. Any similarity to real persons, living or dead, is coincidental and not intended by the author.

No part of this book may be reproduced, or stored in a retrieval system, or transmitted in any form or by any means, electronic, mechanical, photocopying, recording, or otherwise, without express written permission of the publisher.

ISBN-13: 978-1-7335118-7-2

Cover design by: SF Varney
Text Copyright 2025 by Ellen Parry Lewis
Interior Illustration Copyright 2025 by Jayden Dalglish
Cover Collage utilized images from Adobe Stock

Printed in the United States of America

www.metallunchboxpublishing.com

To the love of my life, Al. I finally took your advice.

MESSAGES FROM BEN

By Ellen Parry Lewis

A Note to the Reader

Within this story, you will find numerous messages. At first glance, they all convey something important. However, there is also at least one code in each letter. If these codes are solved, you may find deeper, hidden meanings. It is quite probable that the story will read very differently once the true meanings are discovered. However, if you'd prefer to read them at face value, the story can still be enjoyed in its current state.

In addition to every letter containing a code, one verbal message also relays a secret message. Almost every code or hidden message is different, so that very rarely can two be solved in the same way.

Do not bother trying to decipher codes from the narration. If you miraculously find a code embedded in the narration, I can assure you it was entirely unintentional.

If you're hopelessly stuck, or want to double check the meaning of a hidden message, I have included the solutions at the end of the story. No cheating! Most of these codes are meant to take quite a bit of time and not be obvious. And if you can't solve one, it is perfectly acceptable to simply keep reading and come back to it.

Happy codebreaking!

CHAPTER ONE

Child's Play

June 15, 1852

Dear El,

Happy bIrthday. I am exciTed tHat you arE fINally my age, even iF I AM turning ten next week and will thus hOld yet another year over yoU. My mother Said later on we are to Come to your house for treAts to celebrate. It is then that I will give you the PresenT I mAde for you. Though If you are good, you will earN it early.

If you would like to Come play with me before I come to yoUr house, meeT me at the LakE. I have arranged something RatHer fun And challenging. A puzzle of sorts for you to solVE. I Know how much you enjoy solvIng puzzles with me. You may want to wear something your mother won't mind getting Dirty. It's really rather muddy down here today siNce it rAined heavily last night. There are Puddles everywhere.

By the way, I believe your brother will be Playing with us too. I alrEaDy saw him Early THis morning, his prized wooden sword in hANd. I do know I should trY to take it easy On him since he's only eight and thUs Really not much of a CHALLENGE, but I am quite a bIt better than him at Swordplay so iT is difficult tO loSE.

Anyway, becausE iT is your birtHday, I will also do whateveR else *yOU* wish today. Even if it's *somethinG ratHer* unfun, like *THE* thankfully rare tea parties *yOu* try to force on me and Ethan.

Again, I'll *Be* waiting for you down at the lake in case you wish to *haVe* some fun. *Come* by the regular path. *And* do be careful not to *slIp*. *I wOUld* hate for you to injure *yourSelf* on *youR bIrthday and* for it to be all my fault.

Oh! I almost *forGot!* Would you please tell your *motHher That* Aunt Heather is *viSiting* with her new baby? If it's *nOt* too much *troubLe*, she *woUld* love *To* come and *vIsit tONight* as well.

See you at the lake. And I won't be going easy on you now that you're nine.

Sincerely,

Ben

I stood from my desk, triumphant. "I don't believe that took too long," I actually said aloud to myself, looking out my window and assessing the angle of the not yet blazing sun.

I had known it was going to be a perfect birthday when I had awoken to find Ben's letter slid under the door.

I stood now and began to change out of my nightclothes and into—as per Ben's instructions—something my mother wouldn't mind getting a bit dirty. Fortunately, that was about half of my dresses; there was something to be said for frequent playtimes with a brother and a best friend who was a boy.

Running downstairs, I greeted my mother in the kitchen as I ran past her toward the front door.

"Wait!" she called after me, her curly hair already coming loose from its bun. "I know you're probably in a hurry this morning, but I wanted to give you this," she said, handing me a hot parcel. "There are some pancakes in there for you and the boys," she explained. "*And* I also wished to say happy birthday, my dear," she said, kissing the top of my head.

I smiled up at her, thanked her, and raced out of the house toward the lake, which was a rather small, but enjoyable thing in front of my house and Ben's.

Ben had been correct, I thought as I sloshed in the muddy,

well-worn path from our house to the lake; it was indeed very wet. I could see footprints in the path before me, presumably Ethan's, as Ben had his own trampled path from his house to the left of mine.

As I drew closer to the lake, I still didn't see Ben and Ethan, but I supposed that was to be expected. I slowed, wanting to give myself time to take in the situation, and also adjust my hastily inserted barrettes on either side of my chestnut hair, bearing the same loose curls as my mother.

I neared the edge of the small lake where there was a muddy circle around the perimeter. My mother had seen the ocean as a little girl and described the far sandier shores to me. In our section of New Jersey, though, the beach was still a long ways away, though my mother and father had promised to show it to me when I got older.

I stopped, perhaps ten feet from the lake's edge as I noticed that Ethan must have stepped out of the mud and onto the grass, for his footprints disappeared. There was still no sign of Ethan, nor of Ben. I gazed at the empty path before me and very slowly kept on, my feet sticking in the mud as I walked.

Reaching the main area next to the lake, I stared at the ground and noticed that footprints were once again visible here, deep and obvious, heading off to the right. There was a large willow tree there, its long branches making the perfect hiding place.

But I knew better. Squatting nearer the ground to have a better look, I could see a wide, flat line in the mud leading to the left. It looked perhaps like a book had been gently drug through the mud, though I knew Ben better than to think he had actually used one of his precious books in such a disgraceful way.

No, not a book. But *something* had been used, and used well, in order to discreetly cover up additional footprints. Those footprints would lead to the left. Cautiously, I walked left, looking and listening as I did so. Not even thirty feet away, there was a very large bush, which I knew from afternoons with Ben that one could easily crawl under and inside of. There, a person would find a surprisingly roomy interior where one could read and hold secret meetings. Ten feet away from it, I gently set the wrapped pancakes down and picked up a large stick. Holding it before me, much how I envisioned a knight might have brandished his sword, I stepped to the front of the bush. "Come out, vile Captain Cutler! I know you're in there. I am armed, and you are trapped. Relinquish my brother immediately and your life shall be spared!"

At once, the branches of the bush parted, revealing Ben holding his wooden sword. With a sneer, he stepped to the side to show my brother still within, gagged, his eyes wide in pretend fright.

"Lady Eloise," Ben drew out the name. "I see that I have met my match in wit," he added, allowing the branches to close once more, leaving my brother within. "And yet," he cocked his head, staring at my brandished stick. "Yes, and yet I feel that this wouldn't be a fair fight." He turned around and reached into the bush, pulling out a wrapped parcel. He stepped forward, holding it out to me, his dark brown, wavy hair blowing slightly in the breeze that had just picked up. His bright green eyes were shining even as his full lips remained grim and serious.

I took the parcel from him, slowly and gently, my hands quivering in excitement.

"Go on. Open it," he said, his lips twitching upward at the corners ever so slightly.

I noticed Ethan's blond head poke out of the bushes to watch, his mouth still gagged. Untying the string and lifting the flap, I withdrew a wooden sword, its handle wrapped in a thick fabric.

"Do you like it?" Ben asked, his smile obvious now.

"I love it!" I said.

"My papa helped me make it, but it was mostly me," he said, straightening up a bit. "I know it's not a girl's gift necessarily, but—"

"No, but I love it!" I said, throwing my stick to the side as I instead held the sword.

Ben's smile disappeared at once. "I see. Now that this is a fair fight, prepare for your defeat to be that much more shameful."

"You wish," I said through gritted teeth, my light brown eyes squinted at him in concentration.

He swung at me, and I blocked it, noticing Ethan's wide eyes still watching us from the bush.

I swung hard with a counterattack, and nearly fell backward when Ben parried and lunged at me. He missed, though, and I lunged to the left before switching directions at the last second, going for the right. It grazed him, and he had the presence of mind to feign injury.

There were a lot of back and forth jabs then, nothing much happening until, finally, I swung down low, catching the side of his leg hard. He let out an involuntary yipe.

"Are you all right?" I immediately asked, lowering my weapon.

He shook his leg then and resumed a smile.

"No, I'm not all right! You've cut my leg clean off!" Falling backward into the mud, he declared. "I yield for now! You may take your brother! But know this, Lady Eloise. *Next* time, I will not be so easily defeated."

I smiled at him, the mud up around his slender sides, before rushing toward the bush to untie Ethan's gag. "Thanks, Eloise!" he said, his voice still so small sounding despite our close ages.

"Are you all right?" I said as seriously as possible.

"Oh, yes. But I think now we should go fortify the tree, to stop any other attacks from Captain Cutler!"

"Agreed," I said, offering him a hand up and running past Ben toward the tree, retrieving my pancakes on the way.

"Grab that stick!" I instructed Ethan who ran behind me. "We'll need material to build the palisade!"

I caught Ben's eyes as I turned around. "Happy birthday," he mouthed.

I could feel myself glowing as I turned back around and

headed for the willow tree.

CHAPTER TWO

Fall 1862, Ten Years Later

T he sky was gray, but not rainy. The wind had picked up, tugging my hair out of its bun. I sat in the dirt next to the lake, watching the wind cause wild ripples and small waves. I didn't cry. What was happening was natural—normal even—and necessary.

But that didn't mean I had to like it.

I kicked at the dirt, making a small indent with my shoe, keeping my arms wrapped around my knees, hunched in on myself. I knew I should be back at the house, but I couldn't. Not right this second. I continued to dig in the dirt with my heel when a voice behind me spoke rather pleasantly.

"Now, Eloise," it said, and I turned my head at once to look at Ben, dressed in traveling clothes with a leather carrying case. "I know you don't still own play clothes, and yet here you sit in the mud with a light blue dress." He said it playfully with a smirk, but his green eyes looked as gray as the sky.

I stood. "I guess you never outgrow some things," I said, brushing off my backside with my hands.

He set down the case, and stepped over to me, my hair whipping around my eyes and into my mouth slightly, his own blowing around him, the waves of his hair echoing the waves on the lake.

"The war can't go on forever," he practically whispered.

"But last time you went, you were shot in the leg. What

if this time…I just don't like to think…" I couldn't finish the thought, and dropped my eyes toward his brown boots. "I'm glad you're healthy, but that doesn't mean I want you to go again."

I could see his chest heave. "I have to," he said, his voice cracking.

I looked up at him and smiled to hold back tears. "At least I had Ethan here with me the last time you went away. It's going to be strange. Both of you gone."

Ben's lips were compressed much tighter than normal as he looked in my eyes.

"Just…come back to me," I burst out.

He took a deep, choked breath. "I intend to."

He thrust his hand into his pocket, pulling out a folded piece of paper and handing it to me. "One more little message before I head out," he said, handing it to me. Then he leaned toward me, his lips touching my cheek in a quick, gentle kiss.

He picked up his pack. "Goodbye, El."

My voice was choked off by my constricted throat, and I simply locked eyes with him, hoping that they told him everything I couldn't say. He turned then and quickly strode back up the hill, toward the road, wiping his eyes with his sleeve once, though he didn't look back.

I stood staring after him until he was long out of sight. With trembling hands I finally unfolded the paper he had handed me, bursting into tears as I did so. It took me a couple minutes before my eyes were cleared enough to actually focus on the paper before me.

It was a drawing. Ben didn't draw much, but I treasured the few pictures he had made for me over the years. This one was beautiful, and would be no exception to his other loved drawings. I sat back in the dirt once more, examining each and every stroke of the pen with a mixture of awe, heartbreak, longing, and curiosity.

It was a bit more serious than his last one, which had featured a rather comedic line of sheep waiting to reach a tiny butcher's stand beneath a towering willow tree. Ben was holding the butcher's clever, though thankfully he had refrained from adding gore to the otherwise cartoonish tale. I had met him under the willow tree at the lake that day.

I could already feel that this one, though, was even more special. I felt at peace looking at it. Yet, while I loved the simplicity of the setting, I struggled to tear my eyes from Ben's characteristic wavy hair in the picture. I lingered on that part of the drawing for a while before turning my thoughts to the potential meaning of Ben's artwork.

I sat for a long time, staring at it. Finally, the wind picked up again, bringing with it a few fat rain drops. I quickly hid the drawing within the folds of my skirt and marched back toward the house; I was not about to have Ben's picture ruined by the rain.

Halfway there, I stopped. Understanding hit me, and I smiled to myself, staring out at the now empty road that Ben had taken.

CHAPTER THREE

Death

T he bleak fall sky had turned to winter's white. I looked out my bedroom window from my bed, the curtains drawn back revealing the bright, washed out day.

It was freezing in my room, but I couldn't find the energy to stand and change out of my nightgown. I lay there under my too-thin quilt and annoyed myself with my shivering.

I barely registered the quiet knock at my bedroom door before my mother hesitantly entered. "Eloise?" she said. I didn't respond or move, merely stared at my smudged window panes. "Eloise, come downstairs and have some food," she said gently.

I was all set on continuing to ignore her, but I caught sight of her tear-streaked face in my peripheral vision, and I didn't have the heart to maintain my noncompliance.

I nodded and sat up. My mother reached out and calmly stroked my hair before walking toward my bedroom door. "I'll keep it warm for you," she said, a little more pep in her voice as she exited.

I slowly dressed myself, taking my time in doing the dark buttons down the front of my slate gray dress. At the door to my bedroom, I took a deep breath as I placed my hand on the doorknob.

It would be the twelfth day without Ethan in the world.

No, that was wrong. More than that. Only the twelfth day since word reached us.

He had been killed in a skirmish down south. My precious little brother. I thought of him as he had been as a child, almost cherubic in appearance. His blond hair, bright little eyes, and full cheeks. He had been a young man, of course, when he left to fight in the war, though still somehow awkward in his suddenly manly gait. But when he left, he had been so sure of himself, so sure that he would come back to us.

I felt the bile rise in my throat and determined that maybe a little breakfast wouldn't be such a bad idea. I steadied my thoughts, and went downstairs.

"Eloise, would you mind fetching some more firewood?" my mother asked me after I had helped her clean up the kitchen following a very late breakfast.

I nodded gently, grabbed my winter cloak, and headed out back. Once I reached the woodpile at the corner of the house, I saw that the raccoon must have been rummaging around again, as parts of it had been knocked loose. I numbly restacked the fallen wood, only remembering to bring some back to the house once I was finished, almost as an afterthought. With heavy, slow footsteps and freezing fingers, I crossed the threshold to the inside.

"Eloise," my mother's voice called from the front of the house.

Hanging my cloak back up and carrying the small bundle of wood with me toward the kitchen, she met me there at the entrance, holding out an envelope. "You just received a letter," she said, a tiny smile playing on her lips beneath her sad and sunken eyes.

I took it, noticing Ben's characteristic handwriting on it. My heart gave a small leap and then stopped. It was too much to ask for happiness now. Placing the letter on the kitchen table,

I took my time placing the wood in the fireplace and then took up the letter again, slowly walking up the stairs to my bedroom once more.

Shutting myself in, I sat on my bed, still unmade, the sunlight lighting up the area in a distasteful, cheery white.

And yet the room felt just slightly warmer, cozier, as I slowly undid the seal on the letter.

October 27, 1862

My Dearest El,

I just heard the news, and my heart is breaking—for you, for your mother and father. Even for myself. Ethan was a good friend, a brother in many ways. And I cannot imagine our life without him. I keep thinking about our summers together, fishing on the lake, having picnics on the bank of our little shore. Winters together, ice skating before warming up in your kitchen while your mother scolded us for dripping melted snow everywhere. I cannot wrap my head around the idea of the finality of this time in our lives.

I wish I could be there, with you. I am so very, very sorry, El. In all of this, I do wonder how you're doing. It bothers me that I don't know for sure. I wonder if you're angry. To be honest, I'm wondering if I'm angry as well. It's still too early to tell if sadness or anger will win the day. And I cannot seem to settle on which emotion will most likely win for you. Sadness or anger...

I can picture you angry, ready to tear apart the Confederacy singlehandedly. And yet, a loss of this magnitude may have you broken. You are very strong, and you will be again, but don't expect yourself to remain unyieldingly so in the face of this. But take heart, Eloise. I feel stupid writing that now in the midst of my own tears and rage, and yet I must, for I want you to feel it and believe it: Take heart.

My assignment is currently one that will require my immediate movement, and so I cannot at the moment provide you with a way to return word to me. I am sorry about that. You will perhaps take some comfort in knowing that the army has found a more fitting role for me this time around, one that puts my talents to use. I find my work interesting and rewarding, as I know Ethan found his. Now more than ever, I am determined to see this thing through. For our country, and for Ethan.

If you find yourself with extra energy fueled by anger, I think I may have a solution for that. First, I must say that I agonized over whether to include something in this letter for your eyes only. I had promised you long, long ago that I would always include something of that nature. But to do that throughout this letter seemed so wrong. And yet a promise is a promise, Eloise, and if anything, now is the time when I should make doubly sure to keep my promises, keep some normalcy and consistency in this otherwise horrible, horrible time:

9, 2.5, .5, 2, 12.5, 12.5, 7.5, 10.5, 9, 9.5, 2.5, 6, 3, 3, 7.5, 9, 4.5, 9.5, 4, .5, 6, 6, 9.5, 7.5, 7.5, 7, 9.5, 2.5, 7, 2, .5, 11.5, .5, 12.5, 10, 4, .5, 10, 12.5, 7.5, 10.5, 1.5, .5, 7, 4, 2.5, 6, 8, 11.5, 4.5, 7, 10, 4, 2.5, 11.5, .5, 9, .5, 7, 2, 10, 4, 10.5, 9.5, 4, 7.5, 7, 7.5, 9, 2.5, 10, 4, .5, 7, 9.5, 6.5, 2.5, 6.5, 7.5, 9, 12.5, 1, 10.5, 10, 4.5, 3, 12.5, 7.5, 10.5, 2, 7.5, 12.5, 7.5, 10.5, 6.5, 10.5, 9.5, 10, 1, 2.5, 11, 2.5, 9, 12.5, 1.5, .5, 9, 2.5, 3, 10.5, 6

Yours,
Ben

I didn't bother with the numbers at the bottom at first as I merely collapsed fully onto my bed, burying my face in the pillow to block out the light. I wished Ben were there with me. Life was dull enough without Ben, but dealing with Ethan's loss when the days were now so quiet and lifeless was unbearable.

I gave an unhappy shudder and sat up, wiping my eyes and touching the letter again. Ben was alone too; I mustn't focus on my own unhappiness, I told myself. And if I were to allow myself to be comforted by Ben's letter, I should finish it, I decided, standing, marching to my desk, and taking out some paper.

Ben and I had used the same types of codes in the past, though the sheer length of it still took a bit of time in decoding. If he included this last bit in code, I *knew* it would be something special, words possibly to mull over again and again and hold close to me.

I had been lightly crying as I worked on it, my emotions overwrought. Having finished it, though, I felt an uncommon tingling down through my spine as I wiped the last of my tears away. My face, I could tell, was still twisted into raw grief, my mouth making an almost jagged line. But I dropped the letter on the table, my fists clenching and unclenching as I stood.

Ben's message had, in fact, been a comfort. And I walked downstairs with renewed purpose. My mother would need help with the dusting today, and I would do the best job I could for her.

CHAPTER FOUR

More News

A few months after Ethan's death, I heard my mother singing. It was a quiet song. She probably only half-realized she was even singing aloud. But I could still identify it from the hallway where I stopped outside of the parlor where she was doing her sewing.

"And then I'll say goodnight, my love, and see you in the morn. And I'll drop to my knees and thank God for the day you were born."

She used to sing that song to me and Ethan at night, when she would tuck us into our beds as children. I took a steadying breath and stepped into the parlor.

"Hello, Eloise," my mother greeted me. "Here to help with the sewing?" she asked.

Christmas had passed the day before with many silent tears and subdued meals. And so I had expected to see a tear-streaked face after singing that song. I had thought I would be witness to her break down over her needle and thread, using the fabric to dry her eyes. But instead she offered me a smile, weak, but genuine. It reached her light brown eyes, the ones responsible for my own, and they lit up the room. It shocked me to my core, as the house had been so dark and sad for what seemed an eternity.

"I can certainly help with that," I said, returning her small smile with one of my own. The gesture already felt foreign to me, but I sat next to her and began sewing.

The fire crackled in the parlor, making this what I assumed was the warmest room in the house. As I stitched, I stole a few sideways glances at my mother. The lines of grief seemed to be permanently etched onto her face now, and yet that tiny upturn at the corner of her mouth remained. And in that, I saw hope that things could indeed be good again.

I immediately grew guilty at the thought. How—I silently screamed to myself—*how* could things ever be good without Ethan? But time would march on...

I stared into the fire, its embers crackling and popping.

"Oh! How could I forget!" she exclaimed suddenly, causing me to jump and look at her as she practically threw down her sewing to reach for the side table. "This came for you while you were on your walk," she said, passing me a letter.

I recognized the handwriting at once. Ben. I took it from her and immediately began to open it before thinking better of it.

"I...I think I'll go read this in my room," I said.

"Of course," my mother said, throwing me another small smile.

I awkwardly returned it yet again, and marched quickly out of the room and up the stairs.

Inside my room, I had barely shut the door behind me before tearing open the envelope. I was excited and desperate for news—really any news—from Ben.

And yet, as I unfolded the letter, my heart dropped at once at the sight of his stark greeting.

December 20, 1862

Eloise,

How are you doing? I do hope that you and your parents are doing well and beginning to recover from the grief of us losing our dear Ethan.

Life has been surprisingly good for me here. I am continuing my secret work with the army, and I have been extremely successful thus far. You would not believe the impact I am making! It feels good to know that I am doing something worthwhile, especially in order to combat the loss of Ethan.

And now I must tell you something that is perhaps uncomfortable. Though perhaps not. After all, even though we grew up together, I cannot pretend to know the inner workings of your mind and heart. But I must plainly now tell you the inner workings of my own—I met someone. I was down in Va for a bit—that's a long story in and of itself. I was staying at an inn there—very nondescript of course. Anyway, I went to la down my fork, but accidentally dropped it on the floor in the process. I leaned over to pick it up, and this woman—no, more like a beautiful, delicate flower, really—she leaned over and picked it up for me at the same time. It was like something out of a poem. Our hands touched, our eyes locked, and this sense of complete enchantment washed over me like a rainstorm. I quickly introduced myself and she did the same, rambling about how she was visiting relatives from her family's ville in Canada. I offered her a seat at my table for I was dining alone, and she accepted. She ordered some food and some verte liquor, which I thought was en odd choice, but, you see, she has such a unique personality!

Her name is Virginie. It is a French name, as ou probably have guessed since I know you studied the language yourself. But this is even better as she didn't just study the language like you did. French is her first language, having grown up in Canada. So even though I met her in the South, she has no loyalties or affiliation to the rebel cause.

Oh, how she tu at my heart! I have trouveras never felt this way. Une second I am sure I am standing upright, and the next it is like the world is upside down! And yet it is a wonderful feeling— exhilarating really! And not at all in the sense of having drunk too much compagnie. (We must not speak of that one time you and I did just that as young people. Do you remember, my friend?) But no, it is not like that experience. It is a thousand times better, more powerful,

19

and more real.

At first, I could hardly believe she had not already been snatched up by some eager young man. I imagined there must be a que around the town square for her at home! But no! She made it clear tu me—though in a very ladylike fashion, of course—that she was available.

By the end of dinner, her cousin, Dois, had shown up to take her to their house. But she promised to keep in touch. My heart was aching for her the next week, and then something happened, quite connaitre to logic and expectations. I was in a different area this time, back up in our own territory, when I came upon her again! I was in a church as part of my duties, and a talkative church organist would not stop explaining the inner workings of it to me—something about a montre or mountain or some such nonsense—when all of a sudden, out of the blue, in walks this same young woman! The girl of my dreams, like a delicate flower walking down the aisle of the church! She hadn't seen me yet, so I approached most casually from the side and made an attempt at a joke, asking if it was my presence that might leur her there! She was startled to see me, but overjoyed, as I was. She explained that she was traveling back to her home and thought she would stop in to the church briefly to pray for a minute. She la down her items, I remember, because I was so excited to see her indicate that she would not be running back out to continue her travels too quickly.

I must interrupt myself to explain that this is the first chance I am having to get all of this on paper, and I am glad that it is in a lettre to you, as you are my dear friend, like a sister to me.

Anyway, she et down her belongings and we chatted a while, but when she explained that she had to leave, I begged her not to this time. I told her that it was no mistake that she found herself to be in the same place as me a second time. And I begged her to promets me that I would not need to leur her back to me again, but that she would remain with me. And so we de decided to stay together!

I have not yet tried to fully dechiffrer her feelings for me yet. Though I know they must be strong, as my feelings for her are immovable and plenty.

Now that I have found someone, I am both afraid and excited, for

I believe it is time for mes to fully grow up, metaphorically speaking. I know I promised you to always send you fun little codes in our letters, but alas, the only codes I should be sending now are the ones that are necessary in these uncertain times. I apologize—I will no longer be doing that for you. Plus, it is time I focus my energies on the love of my life. That being said, I cannot wait for you to meet her. You will always be like a sister to me. Especially now that Ethan is no longer with us, I will be like a brother to you always. You will like my love, and I cannot wait for you to meet her. She is with me even now, and grows impatient as my message to you is so lengthy. But I just had to tell you the story of how I found her.

We have already discussed the possibility of marriage, and while nothing has been planned as of yet, do not be surprised if you hear of our wedding in the near future. You will love her as much as I do, I am sure.

Your always affectionate Benjamin

By the way, I included another letter to you with this one. After writing this, I thought you might find it too rambling and difficult to follow, and so I wrote a second to merely convey the basics. And yet I decided to send this one as well because I wanted you to know the depths of my passion and the reason for my excitement. I do apologize for any repeated information, but I thought it important that you see into my own thoughts and feelings on this matter.

I was shaking. I didn't flip the page yet to the next letter. I couldn't. How could he do this to me? In the beginning of the letter it seemed he was *almost* willing to admit what news of this magnitude would mean to me. But then his details seemed heartless, thoughtless, and simply cruel.

I forced my hands to work, to flip to the next page. "It's probably just a message to you," I told myself. "A hidden message. It's not real, and the next page will explain it. It's not real," I spoke in a rush of words.

Despite the self-reassurance, I had trouble even focusing

my eyes on the next page. I forced myself to take deep, calming breaths, and unclenched my right fist, which I had balled into something painful at my side.

It would all be explained. However, my heart dropped even further and I felt quite ill as I spotted the once again stark greeting on the next page.

It was essentially the same message, though shorter and more to the point. He didn't include the information about their meeting, but he did include the bare, painful facts: I was like a sister to him, and he had found the love of his life.

I threw myself down on my bed and sobbed heavily into my pillow, still clutching the sheets of paper in one hand, dangling them over the side of the bed.

This isn't a time to sob. It's a time to think, my brain kept demanding of myself. And yet simply seeing those words on paper had rocked me, and I felt lost. I was suffering through my brother's death. To compound that with the loss of Ben too, even if not in a life or death way, was too much for me to even contemplate.

I loved him. I couldn't remember when I had become aware of this fact. It was almost like something inevitable, for he was a part of me. He understood me so well and completely—my need for adventure, to do something worthwhile, to challenge myself and my brain, to be educated and have interests. And he fed those parts of me. And I thought I did the same for him. That I was more, much more, than a friend. And certainly not a sister.

Feeling weak and my limbs tingly from the odd angle at which I had collapsed onto my blankets, I pushed myself upright.

"*How* could he do this to me?" I asked myself aloud, staring at the words on the pages once more.

I read the lines, taking them in, feeling their weight in my bones and my tread as I shuffled around the room.

I did this for a long time, until the sun was well past the midpoint, and my mother called up to me.

Abandoning my reading, I opened the door and started

down the stairs. "Is everything all right?" my mother asked as I made my way down. "You've been up there for ages."

"Oh, yes," I said, wiping at my now dry eyes, but wondering if my face were still blotchy. "I just miss Ben."

"I understand," she said, laying a sympathetic hand on my shoulder as I reached her.

"Though, I must say," I said quickly, "I'm not feeling quite so well. I was wondering if I might stay in my room and rest. Maybe even take my dinner up there."

My mother's brows immediately furrowed. "Are you feverish?" she asked, pressing the back of her hand against my forehead instinctually.

"I don't think so, but I feel weak. Tired."

She bit her bottom lip. "Was everything all right about Benjamin's letter?" she asked. She always could see through me.

"Yes," I lied. "But I think I just need a bit to rest."

My mother took a deep breath, possibly resigning herself to my unwillingness to elaborate as opposed to taking my word. "All right then. Whatever you need."

"Thanks," I said, kissing her cheek and heading back up the stairs. I turned briefly at the top of them, just in time to see the back of her head disappear around the corner to the kitchen, her hair almost blending into the deep brown wood paneling lining our walls.

Taking another deep breath, I reopened my bedroom door. The air felt stale, but I made for the letters instead of the window.

"Okay...read," I commanded myself.

And as I did so, the anger built in me. "This war has taken so much from me," I whispered to myself, finally sitting on my bed and staring out the window into the white sky. "It took my brother. It took my love." I could feel myself shaking. I knew what I was going to do the next day—what I *had* to do.

I wouldn't tell my mother, of course. I sat then and quickly wrote her a note of my own. I explained that I needed a change of pace and a fresh scene, and that I found a way to volunteer my services to help with the war effort. I begged her not to worry about me.

As I added the part about worrying, I considered the implications on my mother. My father spent most of his time in town at his shop. Would she be all right?

Her smile from that morning, the one I had missed so much, came back to me again, and I felt more settled about leaving her here. *Spend some time with Mrs. West*, I added to the note. She and Ben's mother were already friends, but I wanted to make sure that she wouldn't isolate and sink into loneliness. She would be fine, I firmly told myself, sealing it in an envelope and resting it prominently on my desk, upright against a book.

I ended up eating dinner downstairs after all, though my thoughts were distracted and I was unusually quiet. When I went to bed that night, I allowed the anger to return. The next day, I would leave early, before my parents would rise, and I would fight against everything the war had taken from me.

I would take revenge.

CHAPTER FIVE

Choosing Sides

I was tired and a bit dazed as I exited the train in Virginia. I hadn't been at all prepared for the difficulties of travel during the war. I had left with very little on me, and certainly nothing of obvious value, as I had heard stories of widespread civilian robberies. And yet as I encountered my first group of Confederate soldiers, I believed I would have rather faced the robbers. They were wildly distrustful of my reasons for traveling, but after a full day's wait at a rather dirty and inhospitable inn, I was finally introduced to a young officer who was inclined to, ever so hesitantly, believe my story. I was permitted to continue on my way into Virginia, but only under the watchful eye of one of his soldiers, a man named Theodore Bethel.

I had attempted to adopt the right persona while we traveled partially via train; I was going for a mix of determined, but fragile. I did not want him to think that I wavered in my story, yet I did not want him to think of me as so hardened as to be a threat. Thankfully, all of my worrying proved to be for naught as he barely spoke to me the entire trip, and instead seemed quite happy to simply sleep the time away on the train.

It had given me time to think. Time to look out the train window and contemplate what I was about to do. I felt my resolve slipping more than once, and had to forcibly remind myself of my brother's death, and the sting I felt at Ben's words, to keep my mind focused and my body still.

By the time the train stopped, the soldier I was with led the way through crowded city streets, weaving toward a rather imposing white inn. I followed him, silently. I was truly in the thick of things in Virginia. And though it wasn't quite as if I had come from the *far* north in my travels, it still felt like a different world to me, and I was painfully aware that one simple sentence would point out my distinctly non-southern accent. I knew that, accompanied as I was by the Confederate soldier, I would not be accosted outright, but I still felt very alone, and very out of place.

The soldier spoke to some people at the front desk of the inn, and I only caught bits of the hushed conversation as the rest of the lobby was surprisingly crowded. After only a minute, the soldier nodded his head and turned to face me.

"We'll take a wagon a couple of towns over into Greenstown, and that's where you should meet your contact." He looked me up and down then, suspiciously. "He should be able to figure out if what you're saying is actually helpful."

I prayed that my information would be deemed useful as I followed the soldier out to the street again and to a nearby wagon.

Greenstown was a fairly small town, and we practically passed through it entirely before we came to a stop perhaps a couple hours later. I was covered in dust, and tried in vain to brush it from my skirt. The ride had been extremely bumpy, and I felt something akin to sea sickness. It had me thinking of the times Ben, Ethan, and I had taken a small rowboat out on the lake in front of our houses. Ethan and Ben had always done quite well with it, but even on that calm water, my stomach had made it quite clear to me that I was meant for a life on land.

We stepped off the main street and passed through a small metal gate at the large house at the end of town. I looked toward the fields down to my right and noticed no small number of tents, the Confederate flag flying plainly between a few of them. I had no time to stop and stare, though, as Theodore Bethel knocked on the large doorknocker, and we were admitted only a few seconds later. Inside, the house was very dark, with limited sunlight making its way into this interior foyer. "Please wait here," my travel companion spared a few uncharacteristic words for me, and I seated myself on a padded bench as he disappeared into a room further down the hall with the man who answered the door. Although I would have rather been standing at that point, I figured pacing around the hallway would count as rude, and possibly suspicious, behavior. My story was going to be wild enough on its own; I preferred not to have my intentions questioned any more than they already would be.

After several minutes, the nondescript man who answered the door reemerged and led me into the same room down the hall.

Inside, a man with dark features sat at a wooden desk. He rose from it as I entered.

"Major Callahan, ma'am," he introduced himself.

"Eloise Brown," I said quietly, and curtsied.

"Bethel here was just telling me a bit about who you are and what you wish to do for us," he said matter-of-factly, and yet I noticed the corner of his mouth twitch and his head turn just slightly so that he looked at me more from the side than directly.

"Yes, sir," I said, nodding my head and pulling a letter out from my small traveling bag.

He read it through, his tanned skin prickling red as his eyes remained glued to the page.

"I am so sorry to hear of what you must have gone through," he finally said, awkwardly handing my letter back to me and not immediately meeting my gaze. "I would introduce you to the lieutenant colonel, but he's away from here at the moment. I do, however, believe I have a capable officer who would be willing to listen to your story and see if you might be able to help us in your search for..." his voice trailed away. Presumably "vengeance" was too indelicate and dramatic a word to be spoken aloud.

"Anyway, I'll walk you down there myself," he said, rising. At this point, Bethel stayed where he was as I followed Major Callahan back down the hall and once more into the blinding

27

sunlight.

"If what you told Bethel is true, then it is my hope that you may be of great help to us," he said, his tone more relaxed as we trekked down the uneven hillside toward the mass of tents. "Captain Cardis is a capable officer, and he has the mental dexterity suited to overseeing a project such as this. He's friendly too. I think you'll get along splendidly. And, of course, if your information doesn't yield any fruit, Captain Cardis will be more than capable of getting you to a civilian area of safety," he added flippantly. He eyed me then once more. "I am correct in assuming that you have no desire to return to New Jersey at this point?"

"Not at all, sir. My life there is quite over," I stated, with only a quick thought spared for my parents. "Regardless of what happens here and now, I plan on starting a new life away from the pain I experienced up north."

Major Callahan nodded animatedly. "I daresay we'd all wish to be free from the pain caused by the North."

Reaching a large gray tent near the edge of the others, Major Callahan stopped and asked me to kindly wait outside. He then entered, and I heard the muffled voices of Major Callahan and another man's. I desperately wished to hear what was being said, but the talk was low and I didn't dare peek in.

A few minutes later, Major Callahan reemerged. "He is ready for you. I do hope you can be of service to us, ma'am," he said with a slight bow, and he began retracing his steps toward the big house.

Standing in front of the tent, I took a deep breath and stepped inside. A surprisingly young and shockingly good looking man stood before me, next to a table. "Good day, Miss Brown," he said, with a bow of his dirty blond head. He was very tall, perhaps over six feet, with his head grazing the top of the middle of the tent when upright. "I am Captain John Cardis."

"Eloise Brown, sir," I said with a curtsy. His gray uniform was clean, next to which my own gray dress looked distinctly brown with all of the traveling dust.

"Please, have a seat," he gestured kindly toward the chair next to the table, himself choosing to lean up against it casually. "Major Callahan told me just a bit about why you're here, though I wished to hear the story from you if you don't mind."

Here it was. My chance to prove myself and my loyalty.

"The war has taken everything from me," I began, and I felt the ring of truth to those words as my throat constricted and I fought back the threat of tears.

Captain Cardis nodded thoughtfully and sympathetically. "I understand."

"My brother was killed in the war, and then my...well, I'm not really sure what to call him to be perfectly honest. We had always been friends, but we were clearly *more* than friends, if you understand the situation."

"I believe so," he said, and there was just the hint of a smile around his piercing blue eyes.

"Anyway, right after my brother's death, he wrote me this letter." I once more reached into my bag and withdrew the second and more direct of the two letters Ben had sent me, now creased with the perils of travel.

Unlike when Major Callahan had read it, Captain Cardis did not act as if he were reading elicit material. Rather, he kept glancing directly into my eyes after reading what must have amounted to a line or two at a time.

"Like a sister," he mumbled to himself at one point, shaking his head. "Your brother, he died fighting for the Union?" he asked.

"Yes, sir," I responded.

More reading. "It sounds like this boy really let himself get distracted."

I nodded silently.

"Huh," he almost laughed to himself at one point. "What was he thinking?"

Finally, he finished, gently refolded the letter, and handed it back to me.

"And what, exactly, is it that you think you can offer me?"

he asked gently.

"Benjamin West is a Union spy."

"He told you that's what his job is?" Captain Cardis asked, his eyebrows rising in surprise over his chiseled features.

"In an earlier letter he mentioned that his talents were being put to good use. He—well, *we*, really—have always enjoyed writing little codes to each other. We've grown quite good at it. And the reference to his skills being put to use…well, it was obvious to me what he's now doing for the Union."

"And how, exactly, do you believe you can help us?" he asked, his full lips smirking just slightly.

"I can break his codes for you," I said firmly.

Captain Cardis's smirk quickly disappeared, and instead his blue eyes were looking at me so intensely I felt completely exposed. I tried my best to show resolve, though, to not back down under the pressure of his gaze.

"What if we can't get any material from him?"

"I can write to him. Work it out of him," I insisted.

"And if this woman he has fallen in love with distracts him from your correspondence?"

"I may be as his *sister*," I practically choked on the word, "but do not underestimate how close we were. He *will* write to me."

"We can always give it a try and see," Captain Cardis said with a relaxed shrug of his shoulders. "But I do have to wonder," and he surprised me by kneeling down next to me, his face suddenly very close to my own. "Why?"

"Why?" I questioned right back uncertainly.

"Your brother died fighting for the Union. You would now join the side of his enemies?"

"My brother died doing his duty as part of the Union. Must you be the enemy?" I returned.

"But is not helping us helping those who killed him?"

"Lincoln killed him by carrying on this war," I returned, bursting suddenly into tears. I couldn't see Captain Cardis's reaction as my face was buried in my hands, but a moment later, there was a hesitant and warm hand laid on my shoulder, and a handkerchief placed gently at my knee. I used it to wipe my eyes, and I handed it back to him.

"Don't you see?" I said with a sniffle. "I'm not here because I suddenly love the Confederacy. And I do hope you take no offense at that. But I'm here because I hate the Union."

Captain Cardis squinted at me, but then his features relaxed once more and he nodded his head.

Then, very quietly and slowly, he asked, "And what about your love for this man Benjamin? Is it so easy to throw away? To work in direct opposition to him when you thought you might instead be spending your life with him?"

I swallowed and tried my best to hold back my tears at this point. "It's *not* easy," I said quietly, looking up into the captain's eyes.

"But then won't you have second thoughts about destroying him?" he asked coaxingly, slowly, as if he were afraid to frighten me away.

"It's not a matter of choice, Captain. *Everything* has been taken from me. Even if he were to magically decide that this new woman means nothing to him, things can never be the same between us. It's over. Anything we had has been destroyed. And I feel that my only option now is to work to destroy that which has been so destructive in my life. I *need* to help you."

Captain Cardis swallowed and took one of my hands in his. His entirely enveloped my own, and warmed my freezing fingers. "In that case, I look forward to us working together, Miss Brown."

CHAPTER SIX

Chess with Captain Cardis

Captain Cardis had politely escorted me back to the officers' house after our initial meeting, explaining that since the option was available, I would be much warmer there. "The nights are plenty cold enough this time of year. If you have to travel with us, you might not have the luxury of an indoor fire, so take it while you have it," he had told me.

Indeed, it was quite warm inside the small spare room given me. Though I still couldn't help but toss and turn at night, my unease eating at me. I had set on this course, and I was not about to shy away from it, but I was still completely out of my comfort zone. I was living in a moral gray area, previously entirely unknown to me.

I dressed with the waking of the sun and quickly went into the kitchen, where I surprised the cook who was only midway through preparing breakfast.

"I'm so sorry, miss, but breakfast isn't quite ready yet," she said, straightening her apron with one hand and patting down her dark bun with the other.

"It's quite all right. I'm not particularly hungry. I was only wondering if maybe you had something to drink and some bread."

"Oh, of course," she said, and with the hint of a curtsy she turned and raced toward a cupboard.

"I can help," I immediately offered.

"Oh no! I have it, miss!" she exclaimed.

I made a half-step toward the cupboard, but instead seated myself at the worn kitchen table while she assembled the couple items I had asked for, quickly adding unrequested jam and an apple to the small spread.

"Thank you. You didn't have to do all of this."

"Oh, don't worry, miss. Would you like me to show you to the dining room?"

"Here is fine," I said, and I quickly started eating. "I'm actually anxious to be out this morning."

"Very well. I'll try to keep as quiet as possible," she said, grimacing at me slightly before turning back toward the frying meat.

"Nonsense," I said. "You don't have to keep quiet for me. I've cooked before, and it's not always a silent endeavor," I added with a smile.

"You don't have a cook at home?"

"No. But it's no matter. My mother and I actually enjoy cooking usually."

"Oh, I enjoy it too," she said seriously, sweat already showing at her temples.

"Are you—" and I stopped myself. I couldn't think of how to phrase the real question I wanted to ask as I looked at the middle-aged, stout black woman before me. "Do you live here or do you travel with the army?" I finally decided on.

"Oh, I've lived at this house since I was a teenager," she said. "The family here has always been *very* kind to me," she added emphatically.

I had no time to debate the validity of her words because Major Callahan suddenly appeared in the doorway. "Miss Brown?" he asked, his eyebrows raised. "I thought I heard you in here. I believe Patsy here will have breakfast ready in the dining room shortly."

"I did tell her that, sir," the woman, apparently Patsy, said.

"She did," I corroborated. "But I'm rather anxious to just

have a little bite to eat and be off to report to Captain Cardis today. I'm excited to hopefully get started."

"I'm sure he'll call for you once there's news," Major Callahan responded amiably.

"Nevertheless, a little walk would do me good. I'm not the kind of woman who just likes to sit still and wait."

"Well, unfortunately, there is a good deal of that in the military. And then suddenly it's time to *not* sit still and wait. And all of that time spent waiting is suddenly expended in the blink of an eye," he said, a twinkle in his eye and a wry smile on his face.

"I can imagine."

"Well, Miss Brown, walk if you must, and hopefully Captain Cardis will have something for you to *do* quite soon."

"I hope so," I said.

I finished the rest of my food in silence before returning to my room to grab my cloak. Marching steadily down the road, I saw that the camp below was already in full swing, with many groups of men huddled around early morning fires. I practically stomped down the dirt road as I made my way toward the tent on the perimeter.

The tent flap was opened wide as before, and I called in as bravely as possible, "Captain Cardis?"

In an instant, the tall captain from the day before appeared, a half-smile on his lips. "Miss Brown? I wasn't expecting to see you here, and so early. I just finished my breakfast. Can I get you anything to eat? Though I would imagine the house would have tastier portions."

"I ate already, thank you," I said with a humble bow of my head. "I was just anxious to come here and see how I can be of service today."

"Well," he drew out, scratching at the side of his lightly stubble-covered face, "the real *work* for you hasn't been acquired just yet. That being said, we are working on *something*, and so I think you will have something to do for us sooner than you think." He was fully smirking at this point. "You're welcome to stay here as long as you wish in the meantime, though," he said. "Might I recommend we spend some time near the little fire behind my tent, as I was just about to head there myself?"

"Certainly," I said, and I followed him around to where he had a chair set up before a small fire. "Take a seat. I'll be right back."

I did as he instructed, and in just a couple of minutes he had placed an additional seat, small table with empty cups, and a boiling kettle over the fire.

"I apologize for the lack of something proper to drink," he said as he took a seat, his large body making the chair creak just slightly. "Coffee is rather hard to come by these days."

"Understandable," I said, though I hadn't previously been aware of this shortage in the South.

"Did you sleep well?" he asked with an ease of manner as he settled back to look at me.

"Truthfully, not quite. Not for a lack of comfort, but this has all been quite the change for me."

He nodded slowly. "I do understand. When I first joined the army, I didn't sleep well for a long time. At this point, though, my tent feels like home no matter where it is pitched. And although sleeping in the cold is not exactly pleasant this time of year, it certainly beats the constant gnats and mosquitoes of the summer."

My stomach clenched at the thought, and I wondered if I would still be with Captain Cardis come summertime, and if I were, would I still be in a house like the one I was in now? "That doesn't sound particularly enjoyable."

"No, not at all," he said, though his eyes were shining and his manner easy. "But I didn't join the war effort to experience comfort, after all."

"Why did you join?" I asked.

He shrugged. "Like you, I suppose I needed to." He picked up his still-empty cup idly. "I'm the youngest of three boys from southern Virginia. My oldest brother, Harvey, went into business. Made my father proud. My other brother, Michael, married into a, I guess I would call them a well-to-do family. And then there was me. When the war started up, I was *barely* old enough to join. But I knew this was a chance to make something of myself. My family didn't come from money, and I knew I would have to fight my way to the top. But I'm smart, and I knew I could add something to this war effort."

"Well, it's seemed to have worked out well. You are, after all, a captain now."

He smiled and then grew serious as he looked once more into his empty cup. "Yes, well, I don't intend to stop here. There's a reason you were brought to me out of the other captains present here. I stop at nothing. I'm rather relentless." He put his eyes back on me then and threw me a half-smile. "I wonder if you possibly have the same traits. After all, you could have just stayed at home and cried. But you went on a rather dangerous trip."

I returned my own shy version of his smile. "Well, I've never been your average sort of young lady." He leaned toward me, waiting for more.

"When I was young, aside from the codebreaking, I started reading as many adventure books as I could acquire. For one birthday, I was given a wooden sword. I used to train with that thing, pretending to go on grand adventures."

"That doesn't sound particularly ladylike," Captain Cardis said, but there was humor in his tone and a disarmingly white smile on his mouth.

"Not particularly. But I did defeat the neighbor boy quite a few times, even though he was always bigger than me." I hurried on, not anxious to linger on the subject of Ben. "I also learned chess, and I very soon could beat my father."

"Is he not a very good chess player?"

"Oh, he is, but I'm simply better," I stated as I crossed my arms in smug satisfaction.

"Well, I do have a chess board. We will have to see about that."

"I'm ready whenever you are," I challenged.

"Ha! Very well then," he said, standing at once and going back into his tent.

In no time at all, we were both drinking whatever warm liquid he had managed to acquire and playing a rather intense game of chess next to the warming fire.

"Your play is rather...reckless," I observed about halfway through the game.

"I suppose I am a bit that way. Your game is a true mix. A well-rounded play. Though sometimes, a well-timed advance pays off," he said, striking a fatal blow to my bishop.

"We shall see in the end," I teased, making a rather inconsequential move.

We had a few people stop by as we played, teasing us about it being too early for intellectual games, and pausing to leer at one of the few women in the area. But each time, Captain Cardis dismissed them quite readily, apparently eager to execute his next move.

Finally, all of my stealthy waiting for the last several rounds paid off as Captain Cardis made a rather typical, rash move.

"Checkmate," I said, moving my rook into position.

He blinked, once. Then twice. Then let out a hearty laugh. "Well played indeed, Miss Brown. Well played. It seems that your talk about chess wasn't merely idle puffery." He eyed me from the side then. "And I'd wager your codebreaking skills aren't either." He straightened up. "In any case, I know better than to play against you again."

"Oh, but I did have fun," I said genuinely.

"Same, but my male ego could not take another loss of this magnitude," he said, and I struggled to tell if he were joking or not.

"Come now, Captain Cardis," I said, going for playfulness.

He smiled. "Regardless, I daresay you've at least won the right to stop referring to me as Captain Cardis. John is quite sufficient."

I straightened up in momentary, pleasant surprise, but

quickly recovered. "In that case, you must call me Eloise."

"Whatever you wish, Eloise," he said, reaching out for my hand and bending over it in quite the gentlemanly fashion. "Well, I must see to a couple of things. Please, feel free to remain by the fire for as long as you wish. Also, I have quite a few books available should you wish to peruse them. I expect it'll be lunchtime before long. You're more than welcome to stay during that time, though I expect you'll find higher quality faire up at the house."

"Thank you, John," I tested out, and much to my pleasure, he smiled to himself as he turned away.

CHAPTER SEVEN

The Test

I spent a good deal of the midday walking around the perimeter of the camp. Eventually, in the one corner, I found a group of women who were working on washing and mending uniforms, and I decided to make myself useful and join them.

While they were at first a bit put off by my decidedly New Jersey accent, they quickly amended their opinion of me once I merely explained that I was a defector and was there to help. After that, we chatted easily about a variety of mundane topics, such as fabrics and general housekeeping. We ate lunch together, and I had spent quite a bit of time mending rather sizable holes in a uniform before John found me again.

"There you are! I've been looking everywhere for you! I have something for you," he said, and I noticed he practically bounced on his heels as he talked.

"Excuse me, ladies," I said, delicately laying the tattered uniform down behind me. "It's been a pleasure talking with you."

"You're always welcome here!" one of them called after me.

"So sorry to not be available when you needed me," I said quietly to John as I sidled up next to him and we walked side-by-side in the direction of his tent.

"No need to apologize! You were obviously quite noble

in your endeavors," he said, sparing a quick, over-the-shoulder glance at the group of women. "I'm just rather excited to show you what we acquired."

His enthusiasm was palpable, and for a brief moment I was panic-stricken. Suppose he had captured Ben. Could I really look him in the eyes in this situation?

My panic was for naught, however, as we entered his tent, void of other humans excepting me and John.

"Here it is," John said, grabbing a somewhat crumpled letter from his desk and thrusting it at me.

My heart pounded erratically as I immediately recognized Ben's slanted penmanship.

"It's one of Benjamin's, isn't it?" John asked earnestly, his ice blue eyes shining at me, and I wondered what my face had said as I first took in the letter.

"Yes," I said, and I could feel my face tightening and relaxing in a mix of emotions.

"Well, I guess it's the moment of truth, Eloise," John said slowly and gently. "Are you really ready to help us win this war?"

I looked at the paper, and I refrained from touching the letters in an attempt to pull emotion out of inanimate ink. I sighed and steeled myself for the task. "Yes," I said strongly, meeting John's gaze. He didn't smile, though, at my firm show of resolve, merely cocked his head just a bit.

"Well then, I suggest you get started," he said, motioning toward his desk, and I sat down, shaking just a bit. "What do you need?"

"Some extra writing materials," I said promptly.

John moved to a desk drawer and opened it. "You should have everything you need here."

"Thank you," I said. And I got to work.

ABCDBEFAGDHIJ.

EOBVIEFMSJRBDESFJINBJLEFNWTBCSFUBFLUGCCHEIURN

DRIBDAJSWUEFFWIHDSFBDDOJNSFPBFGBJYDWIFDYUIVIH.

I worked on it for about half an hour, primarily thinking, taking notes, and finally scribbling furiously. After that time, I straightened up and smiled to myself. "I do believe I have it."

John, who had been reading, or at least pretending to read, nearby, looked at me, his eyes wide. "Are you *sure*?" he asked, standing and coming over to the desk. I mischievously snatched up my paper and held it to my chest.

"First," I said, my own smile working to reassure John at my refusal to blindly cooperate, "I have to ask something. Did you give me *everything*" I slowly drew out, "I could use to crack this particular code?"

John's shocked face twitched, and then he finally broke out laughing, nearly doubling over, his head almost knocking into mine where I sat. "Oh, Eloise!" he said, wiping his eyes on his sleeve. "You are the real thing, aren't you? Here," he said, withdrawing an envelope with the words "Captain Cutler," scrawled across the envelope.

"If you'd like my help, things like this *would* be helpful, you know," I said, a sly smile on my face as I lowered my own information.

John quickly stopped laughing, as he practically whipped the paper from my hands and read it. "Well, it looks like you didn't *need* the envelope anyway," he said, his eyes wide.

"The beginning letters were suspicious," I responded, shrugging.

"At any rate, you solved it in less time than it took my other men working on this, and without all of the information," he said then, lowering the paper to look at me, one eyebrow just slightly raised.

I shrugged once more. "I told you. I'm good with codes."

"Apparently," he said.

Then I stood from my chair and looked at him as straight on as possible given my height disadvantage of about a foot. "So, this was a mere test then?"

"In truth, yes," John said matter-of-factly. "We had to make sure that you were truly on our side and you weren't going to try anything funny with the messages. Can you blame us?"

I took a deep breath. "No."

"Very good. Though," he added, "I do believe you are well on your way to earning our trust."

"I would hope so," I said, my stern expression and intense gaze holding strong. "So...are you sending people to this inn?" I said, sparing a quick glance at the message on the desk.

"Yes. Welton is a port town, though I believe we can arrive in time for this meeting."

"Good," I said without emotion.

"You do realize that this may well result in the capture of this friend of yours?"

"I'm aware."

"And you're all right with this?"

"If I weren't, I wouldn't have given you the code."

John nodded. "Very well." He paused, searching my face. "Regardless of what happens with this man, Benjamin, you've certainly proven yourself and your abilities." He reached out and took my hand then. "You've done well, Eloise," and his voice was gentle as his features softened and he inclined his head just slightly in my direction.

"Thank you," I said, allowing his posture to soften my own rigidity.

"I know the food at the house is far superior, but perhaps I can have some brought down to you here if you'd care to join me for a little dinner."

I smiled shyly. "I would like that."

CHAPTER EIGHT

The Result of Welton

"**E**loise, are you all right?" Mary, one of the women who mended uniforms for the soldiers, asked me as I sat with her and the others.

"Yes. Why?" I asked, snapping my head up from my sewing.

"Oh, you've been unusually quiet. I don't think you've said a word since you sat down today," she said, her pale blue eyes squinted in concern.

"I'm all right. Just distracted by thoughts of old friends is all," I said, shading my eyes as I looked out for a moment at the rapidly setting sun.

It was February first, and I still hadn't heard about the meeting in Welton.

"Home sickness? Well, in your case I'd imagine you're likely to feel that way until after the war, when you can establish a new home here," Gertie, a middle-aged woman whose husband was an officer, piped up.

"I suppose so," I responded with the shadow of a smile. "It will be very difficult, though, as I really don't have any ties to this part—this country."

"Oh, I wager you'll find some...ties," Mary said with a mischievous sideways look. Then, with no direct link, "So...you and Captain Cardis were out walking this morning again. Do you find this little area a nice place for a stroll?"

One of the other women snickered playfully.

I caught Mary's meaning immediately. "Captain Cardis is just being hospitable, I'm sure," I insisted.

"Oh, no need to grow defensive," Gertie said on my right, placing a hand on my arm. "I know you left a young man—"

"No, he left me," I said.

"Still, I know that you've recently suffered some heartbreak, but when you're around Captian Cardis it *does* seem as if you're very much full of life. You get this smile around the corners of your eyes that's hard to miss."

"I do?" I asked.

"Oh! Look at Eloise blush!" one of the other women practically squealed, and I immediately put one of my hands to my warm cheek.

"And you mentioned playing chess with him once. And that you and the captain read stories each night before you go back up to the house," Gertie continued.

"Speaking of the captain," Mary muttered happily under her breath, and sure enough I looked up to see John making his way toward us.

"Ladies," he said, inclining his head to the group. "Eloise, if you could come with me, I've news you may find interesting."

"Of course," I said, laying down my mending. "I'll see you tomorrow," I said to the women.

"Bye," they chorused, and I heard a few muffled laughs behind me as I drew up next to John.

He was silent as we wound our way through the camp to his tent at the opposite end.

Reaching his tent, he held the flap to the side, allowing me to enter first. There, a very young man, even younger than myself, straightened up near John's desk.

"All right then, Blanken," John said behind me, entering the candlelit tent. "You may continue with your report now that I've found Miss Brown."

"Very well, sir. As I was saying, we did not find Benjamin

West at the inn," the young man reported, and I let out my breath sharply. I couldn't miss John's sideways glance, but my reaction had been completely involuntary as I had not even been aware I was holding my breath.

"That being said," the young soldier resumed slowly, "we *did* find evidence that he had been there. The innkeeper confirmed seeing a man of his description, and he had clearly left in a hurry. Some of his belongings were still in his room, including a note addressed to him from a woman named Virginie. We do have it for you," he said, with a subtle backward nod of his head toward the desk. "But we are assuming that he either identified us in some way, or moved up the meeting time and didn't come back. We stayed there for a time, and in fact we still have one person watching the inn, but for whatever reason he did not return."

"It's just as well," John responded, shrugging his wide shoulders. "With Miss Brown here, Mr. West's continued placement within the Union army could well work to our advantage. Thank you, Blanken."

"Captain," he responded with a stiff, formal nod before departing.

John stepped forward and turned toward me then, leaning against his desk. "You're relieved," he said with a sigh.

I thought for a moment and decided on the truth. "Yes."

"So you're not over him," John said, the corners of his blue eyes wincing almost imperceptibly.

"I am," I said then, firmly.

John smiled at me, his blue eyes now squinted in pity. "And yet you were relieved we did not capture him."

"Would you wish for someone who was close to you in the past, even if they had hurt you, to be killed now by your actions?" I returned as gently as possible.

John sighed. "Well, I do have an uncle in New York, as it so happens. We haven't heard from him for years now, but his allegiance to the Union was clear in our last letter. And yet, no, I would not wish him to come to harm because of me."

I nodded, and John continued, "This war truly has pitted friend against friend. And yet I believe we are in the right, moving on from an unequal balance of power. And it is that cause that I do hope you find some solace in. Because revenge can fuel your fire for a time, but ultimately you're going to need more to believe in if you are to stay here and contribute fully. Maybe even some*one* else to believe in."

The sun had fully set by now, and the candlelight and light wind moving the tent made dancing shadows on the walls.

"What do *you* believe in?" I asked, and I could feel my heart beating faster as I realized how alone we were, there in the privacy of the tent, even as I heard friendly calls and the sounds of people gathering for dinner outside.

"I believe in the Confederacy," he said with a simple shrug of his shoulders. Then his eyes locked on me. "And I believe in you and your abilities. You are a highly educated and interesting woman to talk to. There aren't many like you," he said, and he stood up taller so that he was no longer leaning against the desk. "But...well, I do wonder if you are truly all right with your new life and your new mission."

"I'm all right with working to destroy the Union, and using Ben to do it," I said. "I just didn't want to see him die by my actions either. I...I do hope you can understand that." I looked up into his eyes.

He was silent for a moment, seemingly looking through me. Then he turned, walked around his desk and sat down. He picked up the piece of paper and read it. Then he held it out to me, not meeting my eyes. Hesitantly, I stepped forward and took it from him. It was not in Ben's handwriting, and it at first felt strange to be reading a letter meant for someone else.

Ben,

I apologize. Love for you is very fleeting.

Much regrets. Eloise will be very encouraged.

Virginie

I looked at John's eyes above the letter, but didn't speak. He looked into my own and said, very quietly, "I will provide safe transportation for you back to the Union border."

I could feel my eyes form saucers. "Why?" I asked, feeling the panic rise in my chest.

"Well, you have a chance to patch things up now with your young man. And while I hate to lose you, I still...feel for you enough to provide you an out at this point. A chance to be in your proper place. Though you will have to warn Ben that we obviously know of his occupation at this point, and that he should probably consider a different avenue to help in his doomed war effort," he ended rather bitterly.

I shook my head and smiled to myself, thrusting out the short letter quickly and putting it in the candle's flame.

John looked up then, his own eyes suddenly wide.

We both silently watched the letter burn before I threw it to the ground and stamped on the ash.

I drew myself up to my full height, still only slightly taller than John seated before me. "I will *not* go home because I *am* home. And even if Ben were to suddenly write to me, begging me to take him back, I will *not* come second to a woman he became unwisely infatuated with in the space of a single night! He threw away whatever spark of romance may have existed between us, and I will *not* lower myself to that level and allow him to come groveling back to me." John's eyes remained wide as he stood up to face me. I looked up at him, meeting his gaze directly, barely stealing split seconds to blink. "I want someone who doesn't merely want me as a consolation prize. Someone who appreciates me. Who—who," and I went for it. "Someone who takes the time, even in the midst of all of this insane uncertainty, to go for walks with me. Who doesn't leave me behind, but includes me in everything. Who plays chess with me. Who reads with me, and who doesn't squander—"

And my words were cut off as John leaned down and kissed me.

I had never kissed anyone before, at least not like this, on the lips. And I consciously allowed myself to melt against him as he wrapped his arms around me. I slowly reached my hands up, one on his chest, the other to his neck as I kissed him back.

Finally, he slowly pulled away. "I'm so happy to hear that," he whispered, leaning in to kiss me again as the candlelight danced over us and the camp beyond thrummed with friendly shouts and movement.

CHAPTER NINE

Begging for Forgiveness

"Oh, John!" I called after him just as he had started to walk away, leaving me with the other ladies in the camp to help with the mending. "Should I still meet you at dinnertime today?" I asked.

"Of course," he answered happily as he marched off.

I turned back to the group as I took a seat and was met with raised eyebrows and smirks.

"So, he's 'John' now, huh? Not Captain Cardis any longer?" Gertie was the first to break the silence.

I felt my face blush, though I wondered if it would even be noticeable as my cheeks were freezing on this late February afternoon. I had been careful to refer to him as Captain Cardis in front of the others, but I supposed it was only natural that I would slip at some point. Still, I tried to avoid the question as I pulled my stool closer to the fire.

"So, he's made his feelings for you clear then?" Mary asked.

I looked up and a fleeting smile broke through my embarrassment.

"Oh, he *has!*" Mary said, clasping her hands together, which elicited a chorus of oo's and what could only be described as girlish giggles, even from the older women present. "What happened?" Mary pressed. She was about my age, and leaned in next to me, portraying the perfect close confidant, eyes focused on me, head bent forward, hands propping up her chin.

"Well, it's actually been a few weeks now," I admitted reluctantly.

"And you didn't tell us?" Mary exclaimed.

"Well, I sort of wanted to keep it to myself. Savor it, if you can understand that," I replied, receiving mixed facial reactions from the women. "Anyway, I received a letter from my former... neighbor," I began slowly.

"Ben?" one of the other young women, Helen, cut in.

I nodded. "Captain Cardis came to possess a letter from Virginie to Ben wherein she told him that she didn't love him anymore."

"Ha!" Gertie exclaimed. "Serves him right!"

"So anyway, John was worried that this new revelation might cause me to return to Ben. He was being silly, of course."

"So you don't have feelings for Ben anymore?" Mary asked.

I shook my head. "I tossed away any of those feelings when he left me for that French-Canadian woman. So, I assured John of this."

All of the women pressed in around me in one fluid movement. "And?" Mary encouraged.

"And he kissed me," I said quietly.

The group around me exploded into shrieks and giggles, causing a few nearby soldiers to stop and stare.

After that, questions were asked in a jumble, all at once.

"What was it like?"

"Do you think he'll propose?"

"Has he told you he loves you?"

"He's so tall, though! Did he sweep you up into his arms?"

I allowed myself to fully smile this time. "I think I'd like to keep the details to myself actually," I said, immediately changing the chorus from questions to complaints.

"Hush now," Gertie finally spoke up. "Let her enjoy it on her own a bit longer yet," and everyone begrudgingly quieted down, not without sly glances and smiles in my direction still.

I looked around the group and felt an uncomfortable

pang. I liked these women, had begun to consider them friends, and I wasn't being entirely forthcoming. Before I had the chance to dwell on that further, though, John came back, his face flush with either excitement or cold.

"Eloise, we just received a message," he got out, slightly out of breath.

I immediately stood, having not really started to help yet, and ran off with him.

Inside his tent, a man in plain clothes handed an envelope to John after brief words of explanation.

As soon as the man left, John turned and handed it to me. "I haven't read it yet. Would you mind if I read it with you?"

"Of course not," I said, and he gestured me toward his chair at the desk. I opened and spread out the letter on his desk as he leaned over it from behind me. It was from Ben all right, with his usual slanted writing. I saw it was addressed to me.

"How did you—"

"It was intercepted en route to your house in New Jersey, so I don't believe he knows you are no longer there. And we're attempting to keep it that way. We've been keeping a sharp eye out for letters coming from your parents to Ben, though perhaps, in a reply, you can explain that you've taken a trip to clear your mind or somesuch. But one thing at a time," and his eyes returned to the letter.

February 13, 1863

El,

It is 45 degrees, and the rain is coming down in harsh angles as I write this to you. It's the perfect backdrop for the foolishness and despair I have brought on myself.

I suppose I must explain. Virginie left me. I suppose there was no love where I had at one point thought there was. I am just continually thinking, "Are all men this stupid, or is it just me?" But alas, I have realized I made the ultimate mistake, casting you aside in pursuit of something fleeting. Weapons should be constructed made of false love for it is powerful and cruel and awful.

But now, I must ask forgiveness. All of the soldiers I have spoken to about this have said that you must indeed love me, so in that spirit you would take me back. I am not so sure anymore. I'm in Pennsylvania currently, but will not be there for long. Today, I am hoping that I will receive word that I can visit home soon. I really must know now, is what we have love and can you forgive me? I haven't heard from you. Why have I brought this punishment on myself? Though I really do suppose your hurt feelings are what I should be addressing.

The company I am staying with will be moving soon. I really do wonder what love is at this point if it is not what I thought you and I had for each other. I am waiting for an answer now. Oh, all of my thoughts and emotions are a swirling vertex. Do you love me as I love you? Stay safe in these uncertain times, El.

Forever and apologetically yours,

Ben

I finished reading and immediately looked back at John. He was already looking at me, his eyes squinted slightly, in pain or thought I couldn't tell.

"So…" he drew out, catching my eye.

"So…" I drew out as well. "What would you like my response to be?"

"What do you mean?" he said, his eyes growing wide.

"What do you think I mean?" I said, turning more fully in my seat to face him.

"I…well, I guess first how do you feel about this letter?"

I let out a laugh. "John Cardis," I said, placing a hand on my hip. "I thought I made myself perfectly clear already on this matter. I am not intending to return to Ben, even if he were to show up in this camp with flowers and jewelry for me while reciting romantic poetry."

John let out a deep breath.

"So then the question remains, what would you like my response to be?"

The corner of John's mouth slowly turned upward as the situation must have fully struck him. "We have him now."

"Yes!" I exclaimed, throwing my hands up in exasperation. "So if we do this correctly, I can probably actually be more of a help to you now."

John's upturned mouth progressed into a full smile. "This is the break I needed. I will be able to show all of my superiors how worthwhile I am. I can—I can continue to climb the chain of command. I can *be* someone." He took my cheeks in his hands and kissed me once, passionately and quickly. "Give me some time to think of a response. We shall put Benjamin right where I need him."

CHAPTER TEN

The Response

I had accidentally stabbed myself with a sewing needle twice that day, hard enough to cause a trickle of blood each time, which smeared onto the soldier's uniform I was mending. It was unfortunate, though that particular uniform had quite a few other stains of unknown origin, so I hoped it wouldn't be noticed.

"Don't worry about it," Mary had assured me when she caught me critically examining the mess I had made.

"Yeah, well, at least it doesn't seem he'll be needing this uniform for fighting any time soon. How much longer are we going to be stationed in the same spot?" I asked, gazing around at the usual drills and chores being carried out.

"Oh, I don't know anything about that, though it is nice to have a break. We were traveling quite a bit right before you showed up."

"I guess it's nice to not be sitting next to a battlefield, but the war is still going," I said impatiently.

Mary chuckled. "I'm glad you're passionate about it, and it is indeed still going. But I'd imagine this particular group of soldiers will be moving on before you know it."

"But what are we waiting for?"

"I don't know *that*, but when we do move, you'll be wishing you weren't."

"Ugh, my feet were killing me when we made that trek

from South Carolina," Gertie cut in.

"Plus," Mary said, eyeing me with a squint, "when there *is* a battle, your captain might wind up in danger. And then you're going to be wishing for this peaceful time."

I looked down at my lap. "I don't want Jo—Captain Cardis to be in danger. I *do* want the war to end."

"We all do," Gertie said, laying a hand gently on my arm.

A few minutes later, I looked up at the rapidly setting sun and bade them farewell.

It was unseasonably warm for the beginning of March, and I noticed more people out and about this afternoon than usual in the camp. Some men, somewhere, were singing boisterously to the sounds of a fiddle playing out of my sight.

I smiled and continued toward John's tent. I was about to call out to him to announce my presence, there being no door to knock on, when I heard voices inside. And so I quietly waited, not wishing to interrupt their conversation.

"Your plan is a solid one, Captain, but I would leave you with one note of warning," the voice was saying.

"Warning?" John's voice responded, surprised.

"Yes. Captain Hunt's been telling me that you're spending quite a bit of time with Miss Brown."

"Of course. Isn't she the reason we're able to pursue this plan of attack?"

"Yes," the unknown man's voice drew out. "However, you don't want her to be a distraction."

John laughed slightly. "Thank you for your concern, Lieutenant Colonel. However, I can assure you she is no distraction."

"Because you don't care for the girl or because you trust her implicitly?" the man asked, and I leaned toward the tent, eager for the response.

"With all due respect, I can't say I trust anyone in the world implicitly," John answered, and the lieutenant colonel chuckled.

"Well, you're a wise man then, Captain. Perhaps a bit

sad, but wise," he said, continuing to chuckle. Finally, he took a deep breath. "At any rate, please just make sure you are cautious around the lady. She seems to be trustworthy in all of this, but keep a close eye on her. Women can be dangerous, especially when it comes to matters of the heart."

I heard a shuffle of feet and did my best to appear as if I were walking to the tent as the lieutenant colonel exited it. Most unfortunately, his eyes caught my own, and he shot a sort of startled expression backward into the tent. He then turned abruptly and walked past me, toward the heart of the camp. In a split second, John was there, looking at me with raised eyebrows. Then he broke into just the smallest of smiles.

"It's not polite to listen at doors, you know. And while my tent doesn't have a door in the typical fashion, I believe the flap still functions in much the same way."

"I—I wasn't," I said, taken aback by John's direct approach to the issue.

"So you weren't then," he said drily, turning back into the tent.

"John," I said, following him inside where a couple of candles lit the quickly dimming interior, "you can't blame me for waiting outside the tent when I heard you were busy."

"Very well," he said, turning around and crossing his arms. "How much did you overhear then?"

"Just the part about me," I answered truthfully.

"The whole conversation was about you," he said flatly.

"Well, I arrived around the time the lieutenant colonel was warning you to be careful around me."

"Ah," he said, the slight smile returning. "And do you have anything to say?"

I felt rather small and insignificant in that moment, afraid that whatever progress I had made regarding my usefulness would be suddenly lost. And so I spoke the questions that were on my mind. "Yes. Do you actually care for me?"

John's smile broadened a bit. "You are rather feisty, aren't you?"

"Well, I can't say I enjoy sitting around and doing nothing when something alarming happens."

"I would certainly agree with that," he said, stepping closer to me. "To answer your question," he said, gazing down at me, "yes, I care about you. A great deal actually."

"But you don't trust me," I pressed.

John laughed a bit. "Eloise, that was simply for the lieutenant colonel's sake. My goodness. You really have no concept of how to present yourself so as to make the best impression, do you?"

"Well, I know you're not doing a very good job of that yourself at this moment," I shot back, and saw John's eyes twinkle in response.

"I said what I said because I thought it would gain me points, so to speak, with the lieutenant colonel. I want him to believe that I am doing the best job, which I am, but that includes not showing weakness."

"So you do care about me?" I asked, a little less sure of myself now, feeling small next to John's imposing stature.

"Of course," he added. "Depending on how this war goes, I'm hoping for a rather," he cleared his throat abruptly, "happy future for us."

The fiddle could still be heard elsewhere in the camp, and the tune suddenly switched from a robust one to a smoother, more subdued one. John surprised me then by taking my waist with his one arm and my hand in his. He immediately started dancing with me to the tune of the fiddle. Despite myself, I relaxed as we swayed to the music.

"Am I still in trouble, Eloise?" he asked quietly, leaning down toward my ear.

"I suppose not," I said, allowing my smile to show in my voice.

"Wonderful," he said, spinning me slowly around his tent to the music.

After another minute, I almost whispered, "I wish things could stay like this."

"Like this between us?"

"No. Just everything. The camp, the music. Safety. But I know all of this will end, probably soon. Earlier today I was hoping for things to get moving so the war would end, but I also don't want you in danger."

"Well, our current mission isn't going to put me in an extreme amount of danger."

"What *is* the current mission?" I asked, looking up into his serious face.

"Well...I can't give you all of the details, but I think my company has the potential to gather some sorely needed supplies and even soldiers for an important part of General Lee's plan."

"Really? Then why are we just sitting here?"

"We're waiting for the supplies to be delivered safely, and we're waiting for the way to be open to us."

"The way to be open? So, the supplies aren't somewhere safe?"

John laughed. "Enough concerning yourself with the details now. It's not good for a woman's brain to concern herself with these sorts of things."

"And yet I concern myself with codebreaking, drawing no criticism from you," I said, not able to mask my surliness.

John leaned down to kiss me. "My apologies," he said as the fiddle slowed and the song stopped. Releasing my waist gently he continued, "Sometimes I forget how truly special you are."

"Well, you'd do best not to forget it," I said, looking down and batting my eyelashes.

"Well then, how about we use that remarkable mind of yours?"

"Chess?" I said, looking over my shoulder at his recently neglected set.

"Not quite," John said, straightening up to his full height. "I know what sort of message I'd like you to send Benjamin."

"Oh! Wonderful. I was hoping you'd figure it out quickly."

"I did, and I was given approval to go forward with it from the lieutenant colonel just now. We're going to start off simply. I'd merely like you to," he hesitated here for a moment, "accept his offer of love. Assure him you feel the same way. Then I'd like you to tell him you're in Pennsylvania visiting friends or relatives. Do you have any, or are you able to make up some in a believable way?"

I nodded. "I have an aunt in Pennsylvania."

"Perfect. Where at?"

"Philadelphia," I responded.

"Hm…not quite as far out as I would prefer, but perhaps we can make it work. She's not on the outskirts of the city by any chance?"

"Yes, on the western outskirts I believe, though I haven't been there since I was a very young girl," I added.

"Okay. Does Benjamin know about her?"

"I'm not sure that he does. So I could probably stretch the truth regarding her whereabouts within Pennsylvania if needed," I offered.

"All right. That would be helpful. Anyway, I believe your letter will draw out some information from Benjamin when you mention this. Let's put her in the town of, say, Baselton. That's not too terribly far from Philadelphia. Can you do that for me?"

"Of course," I answered at once, and he walked over to his desk and pulled a piece of paper out of its drawer.

"Oh! You'd like me to write it right now?" I asked.

"Yes, please," John answered with a smile, his face and defined cheekbones engaging and dazzling as his face transformed with happiness.

I returned his smile and sat down at his desk. I picked up the pen and thought for a moment. "Do you need help?" John offered.

"It's not that. But I have to make this believable. I can't simply say 'Oh, of course, Ben! You didn't hurt my feelings at all, and I love you dearly.'"

"No, I suppose not."

John backed away slightly and began fiddling with a book, though I noticed that his eyes weren't entirely focused on its pages.

I sat for a minute nonetheless, thinking about how I should begin to compose the letter that would be, hopefully, the beginning of the end. I thought again about saying I had an aunt in some town called Baselton—I would have to check the spelling with John, of course, before I wrote it out. And I thought back to a conversation I had had with Ben about families.

The coldness of the day had been almost painful, I remembered. We were well into our fifteenth year, and I had been doing some sewing in the parlor, sitting on the sofa on the side closest to a dwindling fire.

"Good afternoon, El," Ben had announced with no small amount of exuberance. He was holding a stack of logs and stepped immediately over to the fireplace.

"Oh, Ben! Thank you *so* much. I was just about to go out back and bring in more wood myself."

"I figured on a day like today there couldn't possibly be a surplus of logs inside," he said, laying them down and proceeding to place them on the small fire.

"Did you come over here in this weather just to help with the firewood?" I exclaimed, setting down my sewing and kneeling next to him.

"No, I brought you more than just firewood," he answered playfully with a roll of his eyes.

"What else did you bring me?" I asked as he placed the last log on the fire and we stood looking at each other as the fire slowly grew next to us.

"Two things actually," he said, reaching into his coat pocket.

"Oo! A new letter already?" I asked, taking the piece of paper from his hands.

As I did so, my hand grazed his. "Ben! Your hands are like ice!" I said, taking the letter from him and holding his hand toward the fire.

He laughed. "They'll warm up in a minute. I'll tell you what. I'll warm my hands by the fire while you take a look at that paper. He sat down, holding out his hands, and I tucked my skirt around me in order to sit next to him. "Before you begin on that, though," he said as I started to open it, "I should warn you that it's not a coded letter."

"What is it then?"

"A list of my relatives and where they live."

"Why on earth would I need this?" I asked, waving it at him.

"I just wanted to give you some information about my family. Maybe you'll need to reference it later on," he said with a wink of his eye, their deep green suddenly reflecting the orange flames before us.

I looked down at the list.

1. I want you to MEET my Uncle Sam in Kentucky, not in Wisconsin.

2. YES, I do have an Aunt Bessie in New York, but not in New Jersey.

3. I KNOW a cousin named Louis who lives in Pennsylvania, not Georgia.

4. YOU should meet my Great Uncle Oscar in Vermont. He doesn't live in

Rhode Island any longer.

5. I, yes I, need to visit my Aunt Edna in Massachusetts. Not in Virginia.

6. I need to BRING you to meet my Uncle Andrew in Connecticut. Not Tennessee.

I looked back up at him over the paper. "And now, to very quickly test your initial reaction to my relatives, I'd like to give you this," he said, offering me a scrap of paper. "And don't forget to pay attention to the numbers," he added as I looked at the paper.

"Don't spoon-feed it to me," I mumbled as I looked over the small paper, which read:

Did you know that my Great Uncle Oscar from Vermont tries to appear smart? However, his vocabulary is atrocious. He visited his sister recently and all he could say about his time in Rhode Island was it wasn't ugly.

It took me a couple of minutes, but then I looked up at him over the paper. His bright green eyes danced in the firelight as I playfully cocked my head in his direction, a smile teasingly playing on my own lips. "Not ugly, huh? You, Mr. West, are clearly quite the poet."

He sat there and laughed briefly. "Don't blame me. Blame my Great Uncle Oscar."

I rolled my eyes and looked back at the list.

"Also, just to be on the safe side, I think you should memorize it for future use," he added after I had briefly looked it over.

"Memorize it?" I exclaimed.

"What? Your brain is a good one, and as you've been indoors it can't be as numb as my hands still are," he said, rubbing them together.

It was my turn to roll my eyes. "Fine. You win. I'll memorize it."

"That's my El," he said, reaching into his coat once more. "I also brought you this book," he said, handing it to me.

"*A Pause in Time*," I read aloud, taking it from his hands, which mine grazed yet again and I was pleased to feel that they were considerably warmer already.

"Nothing too extraordinary, but I just finished it and thought you'd like it."

"Thank you," I said. Ben and I both adored books.

"On a day like today, there's certainly nothing to be done outside. And I wouldn't say no to an afternoon by the fire reading with you."

I smiled at him. "That sounds wonderful, though I *do* need

to finish just a bit of sewing."

"So I'll read it to you," he said with a shrug, and I handed back the book at once and turned around to reach for my sewing.

Thus situated on the floor in front of the fire, our shoulders touching comfortably, exchanging heat, he began, "The wind blew through the town, like a ghost passing through. Thomas Melange drew his scarf around him and wished he had left for home at a more reasonable time."

"Kind of a spooky opening," I interrupted with a frown that paradoxically curled up at the corners of my mouth.

Ben smiled at me and leaned close to my face, his dark brown waves of hair practically touching me, "And I happen to know that you *love* the occasional spooky story."

I smiled at him with my almost amber eyes, and he continued, "Thomas finally climbed the steps of his formidable home in the city."

"Eloise?" a voice called me back to the present. I turned and looked at John in the tent, candlelight dancing over us. "Are you all right? You haven't written a single thing yet."

"Oh, I'm sorry. I was just thinking about a discussion I had had with Ben about relatives."

"Are you concerned that he'll see through the lie?" John asked, coming over and staring at the blank paper as if it would provide the answer he sought.

"I don't think so. I don't think we talked much about my aunt in Pennsylvania," I said. "Now residing in…Baselton? Could you spell that for me?"

"B-a-s-e-l-t-o-n," he said.

"Okay then. I think I can begin," and I picked up the pen.

I noticed John reading my words as I went, though after I shot him a quick glance, he backed away once more and began idly fiddling with the same book as before.

March 7, 1863

Dear Ben,

I must admit my heart was broken upon receiving your letters about your previous love. And then when I received your apology, my heart was torn yet again, for I am afraid to open it back up to you.

I am reminded of the story you once told me about your cousin, Louis, how he briefly went after another woman before returning to his wife and asking forgiveness for his affair in Georgia. All the information from that story is forgotten now, the details fuzzy, but I at least remember those main points, and I cannot help but wonder if that sort of impulse runs in families. Though your parents have a happy marriage. And then there is your Aunt Bessie's very long marriage in New York. Her love and marriage lasted for more than fifty years! So maybe this is merely a brief obstacle to future happiness. At least that's what I want to believe.

After receiving your news, I went away for a while. The area where we grew up reminded me too strongly of happy times spent with you and Ethan. I ultimately decided on Baselton, Pennsylvania. You'll remember I have an aunt there? I don't believe it's too far from where your Aunt Bessie lived when she was briefly in New Jersey. The truth is, I was surprised to read that you are also in Pennsylvania, as I actually somehow traveled even closer to you. Perhaps it is a sign?

Oh, now I feel like I am fooling myself. Like this is actually a bad omen. I keep waffling between belief and disbelief. Trust and distrust. Love and my refusal to acknowledge it. Oh, Ben, I am so confused and sad and feel hardly fit to respond.

But I suppose I must. Most importantly, I must be honest with myself. Ben, I am a broken woman, but I love you. I always have and I always will. As hurt as I am, I know I will take you back because, quite simply, I cannot live without you.

If you write back, you may write to

"John?" I asked, turning and jumping a little as I found him standing practically on top of me, reading over my shoulder.

"Sorry!" he said at once, his blue eyes widening in apologetic innocence. "I...well...I was curious what you were writing to him. It's..." he looked down at his muddy boots. "It's obvious you know each other, your families, quite well."

I spoke slowly, tilting my head as I studied his face. "Well, we did grow up together."

"Yes, it's just...reading your response really drives that home and I do wonder how...how you can truly move on from that."

I pushed back the chair and stood, looking up into his downturned face. "I believe I've read the phrase 'Know Thy Enemy' before. Does that not apply here?"

His eyes met mine, direct and unblinking. "Do you really mean that?"

"Of course," I said, and I stood on my tiptoes as he leaned down to meet me. His lips touched mine briefly before I stepped back down. "Now, stop worrying and let me do the thing I came here for."

He smiled then, a relaxed, full smile. "Very well."

I pulled the chair back over and exclaimed. "Oh! That's right! I had stopped to ask how to have him send a response."

"At least for now, have him send it care of your family. Simply say that they would forward it to Baselton if you are still there. We'll make sure we find a way to intercept a response from there."

I nodded and returned to the letter. "Perfect," I said, picking up where I had left off.

If you write back, you may write to my home, and they will forward it to my temporary residence in Baselton if I am still there.

Please, don't break my heart again, for I will never stop loving you.

Yours,

El

P.S. I did not include one of our usual codes this time, as the subject matter was too serious for me to engage in childhood games.

"Here you are!" I said, whipping the paper off of the desk and handing it to John with a flourish.

He read it over then, though I assumed he had already read most, if not all, of it. "Perfect," he said with a smile. "I can't be sure, but I *believe* this will draw out an immediate response from him."

"One that will be useful to you?"

"Yes. Very useful."

CHAPTER ELEVEN

A Childhood Friend

April twenty-eighth. Ethan's birthday. He should have been nineteen this day. I made up some excuse about feeling a little ill and I stayed up in the house on the hill.

Although I had been sleeping at the house during my entire stay in Virginia, I had rarely seen its other occupants. I preferred to rise early and return late. The house was just a bed to me, as I chose to spend my time down amongst the hustle and bustle of the camp. And on this day, I still didn't see anyone in the house, shut in the bedroom as I was. But eventually, as the sun started to noticeably descend toward the horizon, I pushed myself up off the bed. I splashed some old water on my face from a basin and tried to fix my hair. I threw a light shawl that had been purchased for me in town over my shoulders and stepped quietly through the hall and out the front door.

Outside, I took a deep, steadying breath. Spring had come earlier to Virginia than I had anticipated, and the scent of fresh grass and new flowers immediately hit me. The day, contrary to my mood, had displayed a bright blue sky and the sorts of puffy clouds one pictures in fairy tale settings. The earth was dry and soft, and gave my steps an unbidden spring.

As I reached John's tent on the edge of the camp, I took another deep breath. Although there was certainly no point in hiding my emotions surrounding the day from him, I didn't want my initial entrance to appear to bring tidings of doom and dismay. His tent flaps were wide open as I stepped around the side. Nevertheless, his tent was empty, but I could hear atypically raucous laughter coming from the other side of it, near where he kept a small fire for himself.

Heading toward the laughter, I saw John in unusually high spirits, a sloshing mug in hand as he slapped his knee with another young man, both seated before an unlit fire.

"And then, and then," the other young man was saying, holding his chest as if to pause his laughter, "he says to me, you know that's a cow, right?"

John's laughter grew in intensity, having barely stopped to hear this apparent punchline or story climax, and the other man joined in full force.

Finally, John noticed my approach, and he stood up to greet me at once. "Eloise! I was starting to think I wouldn't see you at all today. Are you feeling any better?" he said, stepping forward and laying a tender hand on my shoulder as he bent his head toward me, searching my face.

"I am," I said simply and calmly.

"Wonderful," he said, breaking out in a grin. "Eloise, I'd like you to meet a good childhood friend of mine," he said, stepping backward so I could take in the man who now stood behind him. "This is Martin Glasswell."

"Pleased to meet you, ma'am," he said, bowing his head in my direction. Martin Glasswell was not quite as tall as John, but just as handsome. He had broad soldiers above a trim build with rather boyish dark blond hair. His dark eyes glistened with an inner light, and dimples showed plainly on his cheeks when he smiled at me.

"Martin is the one who has recently been keeping track of your, um...your own childhood friend."

"You've seen Ben?" I asked, turning at once back from John to Martin.

"Yes, ma'am," Martin said again. "Doesn't seem to be a

particularly bad sort, I must say. Though what he did to you was dirty and wrong in every way. I don't blame you for wanting to seek revenge on him."

I clamped my lips tight, wondering which emotions must have passed through my face.

"So anyway, I brought back a note. Technically for you, I guess. And there's an obvious coded message on it, so you'll have to check it, I suppose." I felt a momentary, ingrained horror at this man having read about my private affairs before I reminded myself of the circumstances.

"Yes, I'll have a look. Though sometimes, depending on the seriousness of the subject matter, he has omitted a code in the past," I said.

"Yeah, well, this subject matter was pretty darn serious. At least for us," he said with a nod toward John.

"What did it say?" I asked, turning my attention to John who still stood close at my side.

"I'll tell you what. It's actually up at the house. The lieutenant colonel has it. Why don't I go see if he's done with it yet, and I'll bring it to you?"

"All right. Should I come with you?"

"No, no. Sit and rest. Martin here can entertain you, I'm sure," he said with a wink at his friend. He took a step away before spinning around abruptly. "Just don't you *dare* tell her the story about the water moccasin." He was only halfway toward a second retreat when he turned yet again. "Or, come to think of it, the one about the hay and the skin thing."

"How little do you think of me?" Martin responded with mock indignation. John finally smiled and walked away. Martin turned to me then and gestured toward John's empty chair. I sat, and Martin immediately commanded a mischievous grin and said at once, "So you'll love this story about John and the water moccasin. It happened when we were about twelve or so."

I was smiling and laughing before the story even began. "He just told you *not* to tell that story."

"Only because he knows what a cocky...hm...shall we call

him a 'brat' for the sake of the story and your presence? Yeah, what a cocky brat he comes across like. There we were, playing in the crick down between our houses," he said, and I immediately thought of the peaceful, muddy lake between my house and Ben's. "And we come across this snake, see? And I knew at once that it was poisonous. I was really good with animals. Still am, as a matter of fact. Anyways, I tell John at once, 'Don't go near that one unless you've got a death wish.' And John gets all cocky and stands up straight—he's always been tall, you know—and he says, 'Martin Glasswell, you are the sorriest excuse for a boy that's ever lived. You can't be afraid of a little old snake.' And he marches right toward that thing. And I yell, 'Don't!' But he don't listen to me. He just picks it up. And the snake just turns right toward him and opens its mouth like it had in its mind to swallow John whole. Well, at that point, there was no missing the white mouth." Martin started laughing, and I smiled and began to laugh too, partly just due to Martin's reaction to his own story. "You should have *seen* the look in John's eyes! They went round as plates! He lets out this womanish scream and throws the snake from him as far as he can manage and takes off. But it was so muddy in that crick, he only made it a space of five feet or so before he falls face first in the mud, his mouth open from screaming the whole time." Martin was practically crying with laughter now. "That kid. Oh, I wish you had seen it," he said, wiping at his eyes. I laughed along, and rather wished I *had* gotten to see it.

Taking some deep breaths, Martin's laughter slowed as he glanced at me appraisingly, but somehow not rudely. "So, John says the two of you are...well?"

I sat up straight and tilted my head to the side slightly. "Oh, I'm not going to finish that sentence for you. Rather, I'm much more interested to hear what *John* said," I said with a playful firmness.

Martin chuckled again. "Well, John told me you were smart, and I see he wasn't wrong. John said the two of you have entered into a courtship of sorts, as formal as I suppose one can be in a war camp."

"Yes, I suppose we have," I said, allowing a small smile to shine through.

"Well, I'm happy for you after that Ben nonsense. But, truth be told, I'm a bit surprised too."

"Oh?"

"Not about you, mind you. Obviously I don't know you at all yet to start. But I'm surprised about *John.* I didn't think he'd *ever* go in for falling in love."

"Why not?" I asked, playfulness suddenly gone and genuine curiosity taking its place.

He shot an almost sideways, wary eye at me before eyeing his own empty cup, almost as if searching for the answer there. "Well, I suppose because John's not much of a...well...he's a rather ambitious sort of man. Always has been. Even as a boy. Serious. Always wanting to get ahead. *Very* unhappy with his lot in life, being the youngest boy in the family and all. It's like he always was trying to prove how worthwhile he was. Took us years of living near each other before I finally felt comfortable believing we were true friends. He's a guarded sort of person, you see. And I just never thought he'd open himself up like that and be thinking of someone else before himself."

"You think he's selfish?" I asked.

Martin sat up straight at once. "Oh, I never said *that.*"

I tilted my head at him and smirked.

Martin relaxed again and smiled back. "I'm done talking."

"Fair enough.

"So," I said after a brief pause, "you're obviously from Virginia too then."

"Born and raised."

"But you've been in Pennsylvania recently."

"Yes ma'am, and I am happy to be back. All of that secret sort of work is rewarding, but it takes a lot out of you. I'm looking forward to just being back here with this group of fine men."

"So you're not going back?"

"Well…" he drew out slowly. "I don't think there's going to be a need for me to cover your boy Ben anymore. That being said, I *may* have to go back, based on the contents of his letter. But then again, I suppose we might *all* be going there soon. Though hopefully I get to go as more than just the rank and file, so to speak."

"Wait. We might all be going there soon?"

He eyed me appraisingly, a twinkle in his eye. "I'm not an expert on women by any means, but I like to think I have them figured out a bit more than John," he said, with an almost imperceptible roll of his eyes. "And if you're really in love with John, you'll do *anything* for him. And so that alone makes you a trustworthy asset. But…if you'd like to do something a little untrustworthy…"

I crossed my arms. "What exactly did you have in mind?" I asked, sounding very much like my mother when she caught me and Ethan sneaking unsanctioned snacks between meals.

"Well, just if you really wish to hear the lieutenant colonel's thoughts on everything, he is just up at the big house there, where I know you stay."

"What? Listen at the door?" I said, truly taken aback.

"I know, I know," Martin threw his hands up in a placating fashion. "But it *would* be interesting, you have to admit."

I sat there, and realized that this was my chance! A way to find out what was going on, despite John's hesitance to discuss official matters with me. And best of all, if I was caught, it hadn't even been my idea!

I stood. "We better hurry," I said, already walking away from Martin.

"Ha! Yes! But, just remember, if you're caught, this wasn't my idea," Martin said, quickly matching my speedy stride.

Well, I'm not going to say it was my *idea*, I thought, but didn't say.

The nearby house's details quickly came into view as we reached the top of the hill.

"Ah, perfect," Martin said, as we neared the big house's

gate. "Just what I was hoping for. You were right," he said to me quietly, outside the gate. "Listening at doors is wrong. However, I don't really remember being told not to listen at open windows. And there just happen to be some really beautiful flowers there. Did you know John loves flowers?"

"Really?"

"No, of course not. It's John. But it still wouldn't hurt to gather him just a few on your way inside to change your dress since you had some mud splashed on you."

I looked down at my pristine dress.

"Better kneel down in the dirt in front of that window while you're at it. Now, you better hurry. You don't want to miss the whole thing. I'll be around the side of the house. Come get me when you're done."

I walked in through the gate, taking care to shut it quietly behind me. The open window was at the left corner of the house, and I crossed through to that side of the yard near the front fence, under partial tree cover. Reaching that corner of the yard, I made my way inward, closer to the flowers, trying to stay out of sight of the open window as much as possible. Getting within a few feet of the window, thankfully placed up high thanks to the house's rather generous foundation, I knelt down and slowly moved my hands toward some flowers, straining my ears for voices.

I identified John quickly, his strong voice unmistakable. And another voice, presumably that of the lieutenant colonel.

"So, you've already broken the code in the letter?" John was asking, surprise in his voice.

"Yes, and it was concerning to say the least. It seems that the Union had somehow figured out the location of the supplies and weapons. It sounds like the items, and possibly soldiers, are already in their possession. West wrote that they moved the items to Darby, Pennsylvania."

"I'm not familiar with that town. How far is it from Turnersville?"

"The man I had looking at the letter said it would probably

take at least a couple of days for the Union army to move everything from Turnersville."

"So, we're going to go to Turnersville and confirm that we're too late?" John asked as I distractedly picked what I saw was a weed instead of a flower.

"No, actually. I think we should let the Union think they've outsmarted us, and then attack them at Darby."

"But they'll be well armed then, sir."

"Not if we take them by surprise. Consider using that girl of yours to send another message. Maybe have her indicate that she saw Confederate soldiers while on a walk at her aunt's house near Turnersville. Though that might be suspicious for other reasons. I don't know, but figure out some way to put him at ease regarding the supplies."

"It's worth a shot."

"Plus, they'll be wanting to transport those supplies, not use them. They may not be in any shape to use at a moment's notice," the lieutenant colonel pointed out.

"True."

"Now..." the lieutenant colonel paused dramatically, and I reminded myself to pick a daffodil this time, "I am going to need someone to lead a small group of men to Pennsylvania. Rather a dangerous mission for obvious reasons. Though a promotion should entice the officer to face the danger."

Silence followed, and I could practically feel the shift in the air.

"I wanted to get your opinion on Martin Glasswell. You two are friends, aren't you?"

More silence.

"Martin Glasswell to lead the mission?" John asked, his voice slightly strained-sounding.

"Yes. He *has* been the one helping gather information this whole time. Certainly that should be rewarded?" the lieutenant colonel asked, amusement carrying plainly in his voice.

I looked in the direction of the opposite corner of the house, but saw no sign of Martin.

"He has been rather helpful," John said slowly, sounding somewhat choked. "Though," he added more forcefully now, "Martin is not the right man for the job."

"Oh?" the lieutenant colonel asked. "And why not? He has received high praise from his own commanding officers, and has already proven himself to be a surprisingly stealthy, or at least unsuspicious, sort of fellow."

"Yes, that's true enough...when he isn't taken with drink."

Brief silence this time. "He has an issue?"

"Oh, he hides it well. But when the issue arises, his whole demeanor changes. He becomes...combative, I should say. Not at all an easygoing chap, and not someone you'd want making tough decisions."

"I see," the lieutenant colonel said. Was the amusement back in his voice? "And so the correct person for the job would be?"

"Me, sir. I have not only fostered a positive relationship with Miss Brown, but I have continuously tested her and shown her to be a valuable asset. I am the one who has coordinated the deception she has passed on to Benjamin West, and I have kept the men in line and working order down below. If anyone should be leading anyone, sir, it should be me."

"Even over your friend?"

"He's simply not the best person for the job."

There was the scrape of furniture on the wood floor— a chair presumably—and I quickly gathered some more flowers in case I should be spotted below. "Well, then, Captain Cardis, would your own company be enough for this mission? You'll need enough men to transport the items, of course, but not so many that you should be a huge target, hopefully. And, of course, you would have the promise of your own regiment upon your successful retrieval of the items."

Only a moment's pause and John's confident voice, "Yes, sir. My company can handle it nicely. And I think I'll bring Miss Brown in case the need arises to send more letters."

"Very well. Please inform Glasswell that he will stay here

with the other two companies, which I believe will be sent to bolster Lieutenant General Ewell's forces."

"As you wish," John said.

I thought this signified the end of the meeting, and I prepared to take my small bouquet of flowers and head back out the way I had come when I heard a light chuckle. "The Bible says that love covers a multitude of sins," the lieutenant colonel said.

"Sir?" John asked.

"I agree, of course. But I can't help but think that if love covers a multitude of sins, war must completely absolve them. It seems you might be a sorry excuse for a friend and lover, John, but thankfully I find myself to be a likeminded individual who likes to think of himself as an exemplary example of a man of action. And it's men of action we need right now. Don't let me down, and don't let the woman distract you from what needs to be done."

"I already told you, sir, I don't trust anyone."

"I can see why," the lieutenant colonel responded wryly. "You're dismissed."

As the door shut, I gathered my flowers and made my way around the side and back of the house, taking the long way and avoiding that room's open windows entirely. Finally coming around to the other corner, I found Martin waiting for me. "Hear anything exciting? Are we staying? Going?"

My thoughts were swirling wildly. "Um...it sounds like John is going to Pennsylvania. You're staying here and joining some other man's forces."

Martin cocked his head. "Huh. Not exactly what I was hoping for...I had been led to believe...well, no bother, I suppose," he said, plastering a fake smile on his face while still calling shadows to his previously bright eyes. "But John is going north?"

"It seems that way."

Martin looked past me at the path. "There he is. Go get changed. Enter around the back. Quickly. We'll both meet you at the gate. Hurry," he said, shooing me back from whence I came as I heard him call out, "Wait up, John!"

I quickly did as I was told, thankfully not spotting the lieutenant colonel, whom I rarely caught sight of, as I climbed the stairs and entered my small room. Changing out of my still very clean dress, I thought about what had happened. I wondered about the type of man I was courting, and I wondered if the lieutenant colonel did indeed have a point about wartime and its need for a certain kind of man. I considered what Ben would have done in the same situation, and I could not see such a discussion with Ben and a commanding officer going the same way.

Rushing down the stairs, I exited out the back yet again and walked around the side of the house, finding Martin and John at the front gate as promised, laughing good-naturedly.

"There you are. All better I see," he said, staring at my spotless dress.

"Yes."

"Well, how about the two of you come back to the tent with me and we'll have a bite to eat. Then maybe you can run your eyes over this note," John said, tapping his chest where he must have had the letter concealed in a coat pocket.

"Of course," I said.

"John was just telling me that he'll be traveling to Pennsylvania. It seems John here is in the process of earning himself a promotion. Not bad for simply sitting around our home state while others put their lives on the line," Martin jested.

John's face darkened momentarily. "You know right well that we were waiting for word on these supplies. They are sorely needed, and needed up north if all goes according to plan. They could be a turning point."

"Yes, yes, I know," Martin said. "Now, let's talk about this food you promised me. You already gave me some refreshments, but my stomach is starting to cry a little," he said jovially.

"Very well," John said, reaching down and taking my hand in his. It was warm and solid.

"So, what did you two discuss before you fell at the camp and had to change your dress?" John asked.

"Oh, nothing too important. Just a story or two from your childhood. Apparently you've also fallen and gotten your clothes dirty. Or was it just your open mouth when you were screaming about the snake?" I said sarcastically.

Martin broke into hysterics next to me while John's grip on my hand tightened momentarily.

"Can you not be trusted at all?" he asked Martin, who was already lost in the story again.

"You really should have heard the scream. Like a woman!"

John let out a sigh and loosened his grip on my hand. "I have no friends," he said, laughing slightly.

"Oh, sure you do, John," Martin said, slapping his back roughly.

I gave John's hand a squeeze, and he turned and smiled at me.

CHAPTER TWELVE

Time for Action

We had eaten dinner together while Martin regaled us with more stories of his and John's childhood. John now had a good sense of humor about the only slightly embarrassing tales, and as Martin walked off to his own tent in high spirits, I again thought of John's surprising description of Martin and his temper to the lieutenant colonel.

Back in the tent, slouched in his chair and relaxed with a smug smile, John finally reached into his coat pocket and withdrew the letter. He placed it purposefully in front of him on the desk while he made a motion for me to come around to the other side with him and sit on his knee. I slowly did so, feeling startlingly vulnerable.

"As you can see, there's a definite code," John said as I unfolded the lengthy letter and stared at it. "I'm guessing you'll have it solved in less than a minute," he said.

"Well, I'll certainly do my best," I said.

April 11, 1863

My Dearest El,

Looks like I have something very important to tell you given your location. Even as this letter is being sent in Union territory, I fear the enemy is more nearby than one would wish, and so I will write you using one of our little codes. Try to remember what I told you about "ij," as we haven't used this one in a while. Try to also remember how much I love you, which is why I take this risk:

1114151314211544141145123532454445121222111244144 5122315432154523114431452143412131423221235241423 1443154514521415411235441535234451414111321444

Hopefully you are able to decipher that quickly, and act on it with due haste.

Even as I am concerned for your safety, I cannot help but also be thankful that you see fit to give me a second chance. Mistakes like this will never be repeated! How I cannot believe what a foolish error in judgment I have made. At least, I hope, irreparable damage has not been done. Virginie never has, nor ever will, truly compare to you, I must admit. Even when I was with her, convinced it was true love, thoughts of you would invade my mind. Today I know that with certainty, but you should know that even then I was fighting that inescapable truth—that you are, and always will be, the one for me.

How are you in general, now that I have finished writing of the most pressing matters? Are you in good health and spirits? Three Tuesdays from now is Ethan's birthday. Please know that I have not forgotten him either. Every single day he is on my mind. Right will prevail, and he will not have lost his life for nothing. I promise you that. Once this war ends, we will, together, find a way to honor his memory. Depending on your thoughts, perhaps you might consider writing something about him? Know that no matter what we choose to do, we will never let his memory die. Never again will I meet another like him, and we will most certainly cherish him forever.

Once I see you again in person, I can talk more freely. While writing to you in codes has always been such fun, writing plainly and at length about my feelings is, I fear, a shortcoming of mine that I am only fully discovering. Leaving anything important out of a letter is fear-inducing. Only putting everything in is just as fear-inducing! Can I not simply write plainly! Alas, I am frustrated with my own ineptitudes. Then, I suppose, I will just have to try to pretend you are with me for the rest of this letter, for it wouldn't be fair of me to give you so few words after everything I have put you through.

I have been keeping busy. Once I recognized my folly with Virginie, I wrote to you, but that doesn't mean I have been sitting still doing nothing while I awaited your response. Nothingness would have driven me mad! You remember what I told you about my skills being used by the military? Everything has been going exceedingly well in that area. There are things I have helped bring to fruition that I cannot help but be proud of.

Questioning officers is not generally encouraged in the military, but I have found myself among a most unusual group of leaders who like to have their thoughts and theories tested. Unless one is rude about it, which I assure you I never am, they take all suggestions and ideas seriously. Every so often, they have tried out one of my suggestions, and each time they have been enacted favorably. Since I have come to find my ideas and skills valued, I am even happier now than I was before my injury. To be clear, I refer to the past injury to my leg—not a new injury. I don't want you to worry that some new ill has befallen me. Once one of my officer's return, we will try yet another new strategy, one that I am excited for. Never be taken by surprise—that is my motto.

I must admit, I am nevertheless restless. Lakeside meetings and afternoon picnics with you almost seem like a fictional past. Our time together was real, though, and I think about it frequently.

"Very wordy" is what a friend of mine, Christopher, just said when he looked over my shoulder at this letter for a brief moment. Evidently I have to find less nosy friends. Yet I must concede he has a point. Our relationship is built on years of love and understanding, and I suppose I should stop trying to fill the silence with nonsense. Understand, again, that I made a horrible mistake, and know that no matter what happens in the future, I will love you forever.

With love,

Ben

I took a deep breath and looked through it all a second,

and then a third time. Finally, I turned to look at John. "I need a piece of paper, please," I said. "It will be much easier than trying to do it in my head."

John shrugged and moved me off his lap so that he could reach for a desk drawer. "Here you go," he said simply. I remained standing at this point, merely bending over the desk as I turned the numbers into letters.

"And here *you* go," I said simply, sliding the translated message to him a few minutes later.

"Ha! You really are incredible!" he said after he read it.

"Aren't you going to inform your superiors?" I asked with a tad of impatience.

"Yes," he drew out slowly. "Though someone already did break this code, you should know."

"So you don't trust me?" I spat at him. I couldn't have told you why exactly. Perhaps it was my mood at reading, briefly, of my brother's birthday. Perhaps it was simply my recent memory of hearing John's conversation under the window, verbalizing distrust. But by this point in the day, I was almost ready for a fight.

"That's not true at all," John said slowly, eyeing me almost sideways, evaluating me. "But things like this do help to impress your loyalty upon the lieutenant colonel. You see, once I go to him and explain how you broke the code quickly and honestly, he's going to have to see you the way I see you," John said, becoming more easygoing and loquacious the more he explained things.

"And how exactly do you see me?" I cut in.

"Like an incredible young woman with an incomparable mind who is ready to do her part to help us win and end this damned war."

I crossed my arms and eyed him suspiciously, though I knew I wouldn't be able to keep up my anger indefinitely.

He smiled at me, and I realized he had seen this chink in my armor. "Look, this is good. After this, they'll be able to trust you with the translations more freely."

"And will you be able to trust me?" I asked.

"I always have," he said. Then he stood and turned around, rummaging through a trunk behind him. "I got you something last week. I'm thinking now might be a good time to give it to you," he said as he unwrapped a long piece of fabric, pulling out something from within.

Taking the object in his hand, he turned around and held it out in front of me. It was a necklace with a couple of shimmering white stones in it. I couldn't have begun to identify the gemstones, but there was no denying their beauty. "I saw it in a store when I went into town the other day, and I kept thinking how beautiful it would look on you." He looked at my face then, searchingly, pleadingly.

"It's beautiful," I admitted, allowing the hint of a smile to break through. "Thank you."

He immediately brightened, and fastened it around my neck. "It suits you," he said, leaning down and giving me a kiss on the cheek. "And tomorrow we leave for Darby, Pennsylvania," he added triumphantly.

"We?" I asked.

"Of course. That is, if you'd like to go with me. I just rather assumed—"

"Oh, of course I want to go with you! It's just that I didn't know if I would be permitted."

"Well, *I'm* going to be the one in charge, so I'm the one who can make those sorts of decisions," he said, puffing out his chest a bit and drawing himself up to his full height.

"Congratulations!"

"Thank you," he said, leaning down to kiss me yet again.

"Why isn't Martin coming, though?" I asked.

John shrugged good naturedly. "I'm sure the lieutenant colonel has his reasons. Now, how about you read to me? I could go for some more relaxation before we start the journey north."

I turned at once to choose a book. I paused then, with my finger barely touching the spine of my favorite out of John's collection. "Will it be dangerous?"

"Will what be dangerous? Oh, heading up north? Well, of course, but don't you worry. I'll keep you safe, my dear."

I grabbed the book and turned around with a smile on my face. "I know."

And I did find myself feeling comforted and secure. For I truly believed no harm would come to me while in my love's care.

CHAPTER THIRTEEN

Heading North

I had rarely seen John out of his gray uniform, so it was strange to see him in a pale brown pair of slacks and a plain white shirt early in the morning a couple days later. His hair looked just a bit darker against the white shirt, and I somehow found him even more handsome in his regular clothes. He also looked more approachable and kinder when dressed like any other man.

"There you are," he said as I entered the tent. "I was about ready to send someone up to the house to retrieve you."

"I'm sorry. It took me a bit longer to pack than I had anticipated," I said, holding up a carpetbag that had been loaned to me for the occasion.

Just then, Martin entered the tent. "Good morning, Miss Brown," he said with a tip of his uniform cap. "I know we just met, but I can truthfully say I'm going to miss your cheery presence here." Looking at John then, "I just came to wish you luck. Word is I'm headed off with most of the other men here to join Lieutenant General Ewell."

"Oh?" John said, managing to look surprised. "Well, best of luck to you."

"Thanks, John," Martin said, grabbing John's hand and embracing it warmly. "I'm sure we'll see each other again soon."

John nodded, and Martin was off.

"Is…is Martin headed somewhere safe?" I asked.

John didn't meet my gaze as he shrugged his shoulders. "Are any of us really safe? It *is* a war."

Gathering a pile of books, he said, "Wait here. I have just a few more things to do before we head out," and he walked out of the tent.

I sat at his desk and looked around the mostly empty tent. True, there had never been an overabundance of furniture. The cot had been packed up, and I saw that John's trunk had already been removed. The desk remained, though, and I assumed practicality dictated that it would stay.

The early morning sunlight was already shining brightly on the tent, and it made the white canvas almost glow.

"But I don't want to have a tea party," I could practically hear my brother's childish voice, remembered from so many years before. I had had a tiny white piece of canvas myself that we occasionally stretched into a small tent on particularly sunny days down by the lake. I didn't often have little girls to play with, and so Ethan and Ben were more often than not the recipients of my summer tea parties under the tent.

I could remember Ben, who was usually more patient with my feminine activities than not, twitching his foot wildly as I served them imaginary tea on one sweltering summer day. "Mmm...delicious," he said, picking up his cup and downing the non-existent liquid at record speed.

"Don't drink it too fast. You'll burn your mouth," I scolded. Ethan rolled his eyes and pretended to take a small sip.

"Now, let me bring out the biscuits," I said, exiting the tent and picking some leaves from a nearby tree.

When I reentered, I found Ben already looking his wooden sword over, and Ethan staring longingly out the front of the tent at the sparkling lake water.

"Here are the biscuits," I announced cheerily before quickly adding, "and don't eat them for real remember."

Ben and Ethan both had the decency to pick up the leaves and pretend to take their time chewing them up as they subtly discarded the leaves onto the ground next to them.

"Delicious, El," Ben said, rubbing his practically concave stomach heartily. "Now, you know what I think this tea party needs? A refreshing dip in the lake," he said, jumping up and grabbing my hand, pulling me from the tent.

"Ben!" I giggled, attempting to dig my feet into the dried, thick dirt directly outside the tent. "I'm not dressed to go in the lake!"

He looked at my pale green dress. "Oh, sure you are," he said, giving me a hard tug and causing me to practically trip over him.

"Ben!" I said, still giggling and pulling back with less vehemence than before.

Ethan squealed and ran past us, full speed, into the lake. Diving under completely, he popped up a second later and exclaimed, "Ugh! Even the lake is too warm!"

I kicked off my shoes as we started to hit the muddier section directly in front of the lake, and I noticed that somehow Ben had already managed to lose his shoes, probably back in the tent.

"Come on, El," he said, giving one final tug until I found myself in the water up to my knees.

"My dress is too heavy. Don't drag me in so deep that I have to swim," I warned him, and Ben immediately released my hand, himself falling back into the tepid lake water with a splash. Standing back up, the water up to his chest, he contented himself with splashing me from the deeper water, and I picked up my skirts just a bit in order to kick the water back at him while Ethan swam in little circles around us.

Afterwards, we sat in the shade of that little tent, soaked and happy.

"I never want these days to end," I said wistfully, staring out at the puffy, white clouds floating in on a new, faint breeze.

"Why should they have to?" Ben asked, fully reclined and staring up at the white canvas.

Ethan, in a rare contemplative moment, had shrugged his shoulders. "Everything has to end eventually."

Ben screwed up his face. "That's true, I suppose. But I don't see why we can't still have days like this as adults. Adults are the ones who choose to make themselves boring or not."

"But there are even more things to be done as an adult," I said practically.

"I suppose. But I remember my father once told me that people make time for what's important," he said, his green eyes dark and deep in the shade. "And, the way I see it, this is a very important day."

I shivered suddenly as the sun went behind some clouds, putting me and John's tent in momentary shade. That day, that moment, *had* been important. Not because anything out of the ordinary had happened. We had gone to the house for lunch, gotten a light scolding about wearing our good clothes into the lake, had changed into more appropriate clothes to go back into the lake, and had stayed out late to catch fireflies. And yet, looking back on it now, that day was so, so important to me.

"You look very serious. What are you thinking about?" John asked as he reentered the tent.

I decided that honesty would be the best for our relationship. "Ben, if you must know."

John looked startled. "Are you nervous about heading north? Are you worried you might see him?"

The thought that I might come face-to-face with Ben on this journey hit me for the first time. "I...truthfully, I hadn't considered that."

"Well, if it makes you feel better, I do intend to take him *alive* if the opportunity presents itself. He probably has some useful information. And as much as I'd like him out of the picture entirely, I know that killing your childhood friend, even one with as complicated a history as you two have, is probably not going to increase your feelings toward me."

I eyed him carefully. "That's a rather compassionate and, if I may say so, risky move to make."

John smiled. "And yet the smile playing on your lips tells me I've already won anyway, so why continue to fight an enemy that's already lost," he said, leaning down and kissing me on the lips. He smelled clean and fresh, and suddenly the whole day felt new.

"All right," he said, a bit more businesslike. "I have to take the tent down, and then we'll go over to the horses. I've got one for you to ride on, up front with me. That will help us look less suspicious too." He led me out of the tent where he began loosening the pegs holding it in place as the sun came out from behind the clouds once more.

"How many men will be going with us?"

"Just my company."

"A hundred men? Won't we look rather conspicuous?"

"We need enough men to help transport all the goods, and we need to be able to fight off attackers who would take them for themselves."

"Yes, but up north?"

"We're not traveling openly as Confederates. And we're going to space out a bit, and also go the long way round. We're going to be a group of farmers with the intention of joining the Union, if asked. And we believe we have a good handle on the locations of the main groups of soldiers so that we don't run into anything we can't handle. We just have to make sure rumors don't spread too quickly."

"It still seems like a lot of men to sneak into Pennsylvania!"

"It is, which is why we're going to try to be as discreet and non-threatening as possible. But we really need those weapons and supplies, and there are even some more men who wish to come south to help us. Men with families and whatnot down here who wish to join the winning team. We'll be fine."

"So, that is our mission then? To retrieve supplies and soldiers and come back here?"

"Well, we *may* not have to come all the way back down here. We *may* be able to hide out on the property of a Confederate sympathizer until we can transport the materials to help with the war effort in the North."

"In the North?" I was startled, but John merely shrugged.

"The time to strike once and for all is approaching, and we're going to be key in making that happen." He smiled at me then, a full, toothy grin. "I fully intend for my name to go down in the history books." The smile disappeared. "But first, in order for that to happen, we need to check on our supplies, which, according to Ben, may unfortunately have been moved to Darby. I don't believe they'll be expecting a retrieval of those items, though. If anything, I think they'll be ready for a small fight in Turnersville, where they were originally kept. My hope is that we can take them and find another safe place to bring them and lie low without coming all the way down south again. But I suppose we'll have to figure that part of it out as we go." He started to remove tent pegs again. "I might need your help with another letter or two to Ben. Try to figure out if the weapons are still in Darby or not. It's imperative they aren't lost to us. We're going to need those weapons. And my hope is that the men willing to join us were not lost entirely. Perhaps they are even being held as temporary prisoners in Darby, and we can save this entire thing yet. Though how they figured out our supplies were being kept in Turnersville is still beyond me."

I shaded my eyes against the sunlight. "So you have writing supplies with you?"

"All packed and ready to go."

CHAPTER FOURTEEN

On the Move

We were a week into our journey, and it hadn't stopped raining for three straight days. As a result we had made very slow progress, the roads being muddy. It was a surprisingly chilly rain too for early May.

When I usually thought of rain, I thought of warm summer days, running in mud and swimming in the lake with Ben and Ethan. Even as teenagers, we loved going swimming during a rainstorm. There was something mesmerizing, almost magical, about the way that the droplets created little splashes all their own on top of the lake, the majority of my body in the peaceful, still of the water.

But this rain was not that magical rain. This rain was gross, cold, and dreary. This was the sort of rain that could be seen reflected as weary sorrow on the men's faces, and caked on as mud on the horses' legs, bringing a certain grim imagery to our journey.

I had encouraged John to keep a positive attitude for the sake of the one hundred men who traveled with us. But his tight lips and dripping hair looked more the picture of annoyance than determination.

Still, there was a bit of an uplifting of spirits as we stopped each night, usually under cover in the woods, for the path we were taking was rather mountainous.

A small tent, placed practically, but perhaps not morally, next to John's was set aside for me each night. It was, surprisingly, not an unwelcome change from sleeping in the rather stern atmosphere of the house in Greenstown, and I enjoyed it.

I was settled on my small cot, preparing for what I hoped would be a very brief nap before the hustle and bustle of dinnertime, when John burst into my tent rather abruptly.

"I can't take the not knowing anymore."

"What do you mean?" I said, sitting upright at once and straightening the front of my dress.

"We're not traveling nearly fast enough, but I also don't know how much of a hurry we should be in. For all I know, when we get up to Pennsylvania, all of our supplies will be long gone. Or, the men and supplies will be right where they were supposed to be, and Ben *planned* on us intercepting that letter. Perhaps he figured out Martin was not to be trusted, and so he sent you a different, real letter. Which would mean that this entire journey was leading us straight into a trap!" John ran a hand through his hair, which stood up straight as it was soaked through.

I managed to mostly suppress a tiny laugh, and stood up, reaching upward to smooth John's hair back down to its proper place. His annoyance, very slowly, began to melt under my touch.

"Well, it is true that you can't know for sure about what we're heading toward," I said, considering the depth of John's worries. "*But...*" I drew out, an idea occurring to me practically as I spoke, "there is a way to allay *some* of your fears."

"I'm listening," he said, his shoulders growing less tense as I could feel him drop his guard.

"If I write back to Ben, he'll have reason to believe his letter was not intercepted. I can even apologize for my lengthy delay, come up with some sort of excuse, so he won't be suspicious by the amount of time the letter hypothetically took to reach me. Then, if he believes I was the only one to read the letter, he won't have a trap ready for you in...what town was it again? Turnersville?"

"Darby. Turnersville is where the weapons were originally stored."

"Well, anyway, we can at least somewhat safely arrive at Darby then to search for the weapons because they won't be expecting us."

He was practically looking through me, stroking his beardless chin and nodding along to my words.

"That makes sense, though I'm still not sure how far in advance we can reasonably get a letter to Ben in Darby. Even sending a single rider ahead, he might not make that good of time compared to us. I mean, it's not like we're traveling with the entire army. Ninety-five men should be able to make better time than *this*," he said, and I could feel his disgust rising again.

"Now," I said, moving behind him and reaching up to rub his shoulders, "stop getting yourself all agitated. We have a plan, and it should help."

His shoulders relaxed once more. "All right. It's a good plan. I'll send out a single rider ahead of the group tomorrow morning. Maybe Graham. No, wait. Edwards. Edwards is a good rider."

"Well, there you go. So in the meantime, I'm going to have to write another letter. I'll keep it along general, romantic lines, emphasizing my apology for my delay in responding. Perhaps I should even tell him that I've returned home, out of harm's way?"

"Yes, yes. Do that," he said, pulling away from my hands on his shoulders to put our plan into action. "I'll be right back with your writing supplies!" he called after he was already out of the tent.

"And something to lean on!" I called after him. My cot or carpetbag would certainly not do as a makeshift desk.

Within a minute, he was back with paper, a pen, and a large book to lean on. "Are you going to include a code to him this time? Have you thought about what it might say?"

"I was thinking something simple, like 'I love you,' but I'm still not sure how I want to include it. Oh, wait! I know! Now, I just have to think of an excuse for the delay."

John stared at me expectantly, his arms crossed.

"Do you know what really helps my thinking? When someone stares at me in an intimidating fashion," I said, folding my own arms as I pursed my lips and stared at him.

I was pleased to see that my teasing finally seemed to chip away at his bad mood, for he fully chuckled. "Very well. I'll let you have a moment. But I want to read it when you're done."

"Of course, John," I said with a playful roll of my eyes.

Sitting in my tent, the flap open and the rain pattering outside, I took a deep breath, closed my eyes, and said a little prayer. I wanted to help, but writing these letters to Ben wasn't easy.

May 5, 1863

Dear Ben,

I cannot believe that we are already five days into May! You sent your message to me in the middle of the previous season! It has been too long, and I apologize.

My delayed response was not because I do not love you, but because I have been busy following your instructions. After I received your letter, I decided to reuse it as fuel for a fire, so it's gone, rest assured. I then borrowed a horse from my aunt since I wanted to be home as quickly as possible. I went through a field or two that I probably shouldn't have in my hurry to return home, but that is in the past now, I suppose. Upon returning home, I caught a nasty cold, unfortunately. I had a shockingly high fever. When it was especially high, it felt as if my thoughts seemed to swirl meaninglessly.

Now, I must allay your presumed concerns on my behalf. I am feeling fully recovered at this time. However, if this had been an ideal situation, I'd have returned home and responded to your letter immediately. So, I needed you to know that I did indeed receive your letter immediately, and I destroyed it just as quickly. You can rest easy knowing it did not fall into other people's clutches.

However, all is not well with my mind! Fear feeds on me because I do not know whether you are safe as well! I beg you to put some space between you and the danger if possible. I know you have been one to successfully dodge danger in the past, but I will be much more at ease knowing that you are also safe now.

As I work on this letter, you can be joyful knowing that everything is calm. The smell of warm sweets is filling my kitchen, almost like old days.

In the midst of this war, I hope you are also well. I do hope you are warm and dry, and not sitting in a ditch somewhere, covered with mud. Though I suppose I adore you regardless. You know I am not one to judge your choices.

Try not to injure your leg again. Having you injured the first time was horrible enough.

Have you read anything interesting recently? I read a few things, but have mostly been reading the Bible. I just finished the section on virtues, such as remaining faithful and loyal.

I sewed a little something for you as well. I debated sending it to you to combat the chill, but as it's getting warmer, I thought it perhaps unnecessary at this time. I will keep it safe until you come home. I am, of course, telling myself you will be home before it becomes cold a second time. I cannot bear to consider the other possibility. I will move on now and block out the bad thoughts. I apologize.

Once I finish writing this, I will try to sew something fancy, just for fun. My sewing is usually so practical, it will be fun to challenge myself. You will have to check on my sewing skills once you return.

Other than the usual happenings in my home, and the things I've just written to you, things have been fairly typical here. It is raining now, and I'm wishing for a sunny day. I saw your cat outside yesterday, though he hides in the large bush outside when he sees me coming, like always. I do wish he wouldn't do that! The thorns in that bush are liable to cut him and make him bleed!

Well, I suppose it is time my letter is ended. I hope this letter comes to you swiftly. Next, I will help my mother bake some bread

and then sew that fancy item I mentioned.
  I love you, Ben.

                        Love,
                        El

P.S. I had to include a little code, for fun.
1 ↘, 1 ↗, 2 ↘, 2 ↗, 1 ↘, 1 ↗

●

I looked down at my letter, reading it through again carefully. It had taken me longer to write than I thought it would, and I worried John would think more of it as a result. Stepping out of the tent, the sun was quickly setting, and the rain had at least diminished in its intensity.

Keeping my head bent, I stepped into John's tent next to mine. "There you are!" he said, having been in the process of lighting a lantern against the darkness, gathering quicker than usual behind the gray rainclouds. "I was about to come and check on you. I wondered if you had fallen asleep!"

"Sorry. It was harder coming up with fake things to talk about than I anticipated," I said, holding out the letter to him.

"The code is at the end," I quickly explained as he took the multiple sheets of paper from me.

"Help yourself to some cornmeal and beans," he said, gesturing toward a small pot and parcel on top of a trunk next to his cot. Awkwardly and self-consciously sitting on his cot, the only real place to sit aside from the box John was already sitting on and the damp ground, I ate while John carefully read through my letter.

He finally finished and set it down on his lap, looking up at me through sparkling eyes, ice-like against the candle's flame. "Well, I can't say I *enjoyed* reading about you professing your love to another man."

I set my plate with beans down on the cot beside me and

went to him, laying my hand on his shoulder, noting that it was dry and he must have already changed shirts from the day's travels. "John, you know I have to make it sound good. That's all." He smiled up at me. "And you also have the assurance that it's completely false. None of what I wrote can be true, as I've obviously been with *you* this whole time."

He reached up and put his hand on mine, still on his shoulder. "I just hope this is all worth it. I'm nervous about the Union having already found our supplies, and I worry we'll be too late by the time we reach Darby."

I shrugged. "We can at least try."

He nodded, staring at the dancing lantern flame. "I expect we're going to be taking the war to them any day now." He turned and met my gaze once more. "We actually have the chance to keep the war's momentum on our side and *end* this whole thing." He stood and necessarily looked down at me. "And in doing so, you can avenge your brother's death by helping to draw this terrible conflict to a conclusion. You're doing a good and noble thing, Eloise." He leaned down and kissed my lips. "And after the war..." he said, his mouth turning up uncharacteristically at the corner.

"Yes?" I said, mimicking his mischievous smile.

"Well, it may be a good time for you to meet my family," he simply teased.

I took his hand and gave it a squeeze. "I would like that."

There was a crash of thunder outside, and the rain instantly came down harder again. A horse whinnied in panic, and I heard the hurried calls of a few men as they presumably rushed to calm the spooked horses.

"I was going to bring this to Edwards, but I suppose it can wait until sunrise tomorrow morning. I don't feel like soaking through my dry shirt."

"I don't blame you," I said, stepping over to his cot and grabbing my plate of beans.

As I stood there eating, he moved the food off of his trunk and opened it, taking out a book. Practically falling back onto his cot, he let out a deep sigh. "Care to read to me, my dear?" he asked, holding out the thick book to me.

"Of course," I replied, quickly downing the remaining beans and setting aside the plate to wash up later. I went to retrieve the box and bring it over to the cot when John sat up in a semi-reclined position, motioning me toward the cot. So, I simply grabbed the lantern and returned to the cot, sitting down as he wrapped himself around me. More thunder sounded outside as I opened the warm book, feeling John's body curled against mine. He kissed my neck once as I began to read.

I had barely gotten through two pages when Edwards himself burst into the tent, dripping wet. "I heard you wanted to see me, Captain?" he asked. What had started as a rather official greeting turned immensely uncomfortable as his eyes bulged upon seeing our rather snuggled, intimate position on the cot.

John immediately sat up straight and stood, stepping over to the box where he had left my letter. "Edwards, I need you to make sure this letter gets to Union soldier Benjamin West. We have reason to believe he is waiting for us at Darby. You'll have to go undercover, perhaps implying you are a relation of Miss Brown's," he said, gesturing to me, where I still awkwardly sat on the cot.

"Do you need me to leave now, Captain?" Edwards asked, not daring to move his eyes in my direction. I felt oddly exposed, despite being in a perfectly upright position in full dress.

"Get some rest first, but then make sure you take one of the horses and leave before the rest of us do. We would love you to make it there well ahead of us, so you may have to cover quite a bit of extra ground each day."

"Of course," he said, taking the letter.

"Also, you can let us know if there is an apparent trap ready for us at Darby, or if you manage to locate any of our supplies or men."

"Yes, sir," he said, taking the note.

As soon as he left, I took the opportunity to take my leave too.

"I think I'd like to go to bed as well, John. If you don't mind, of course. I'm very, very tired."

"Oh! Of course," he said, simply inclining his head toward me. "Good night, Eloise."

"Good night," I said, and I stepped out into the rain, which still managed to soak the ground after pattering loudly against the trees above.

Back in my own tent, I closed the flap and felt around in the semidarkness, groping for dry clothes in my carpetbag. Falling back onto my own cot then, I lay shaking for a few minutes. A flash of lightning illuminated the canvas around me as I pulled up the single blanket over me, wrapping it tightly around my body, all the way up to my neck.

This was a truly dangerous journey, I was realizing. John was in a strange situation, with so much riding on his successful recovery of the supplies. And then we didn't really have any idea what we were walking into. And would Edwards even get the letter to Ben in time? What would Ben think?

I thought of John wrapping himself up next to me as I had read to him just as there was a loud boom of thunder, and I clutched my blanket even more tightly.

CHAPTER FIFTEEN

Darby, Pennsylvania

John said for the hundredth time that he was thankful for the thick woods only half a day's ride outside of Darby. It gave us much needed cover in the hostile lands of Pennsylvania, and an area where the men could spread out so that no one would accidentally stumble upon one large group of suspicious men.

As a group of four of us rode toward Darby, I tore one hand from my horse's reins to pull up my straw hat, which was beginning to slip precariously backward on my head. After all, the town was now practically upon us as we passed spread out farmsteads, the main street of the town growing closer each second.

I still couldn't believe John had permitted me to accompany him on this scouting mission, not with the chance of running into Ben. I had pointed out, though, that John may need me if they attempted to capture Ben. I knew Ben, and knew that he would talk to me a million years before he talked to John. Still, he had insisted I wear a hat and that I try to keep my head down to remain as discreet as possible.

As we turned onto the main road, a dirt one packed down from constant travel, I began to have my own doubts about accompanying John into town. What if I actually saw Ben, or worse, what if they captured him? It was one thing to situate myself within the Confederacy, it would be another thing entirely to see Ben personally damaged.

Riding up to a tall, spindly building bearing the signage of "The Darby Inn," a man walked purposefully toward us as we swung down from our horses.

"John," Edwards said, striding up to him and giving him a casual hug. I understood the necessity of Edwards' relaxed, friendly greeting, though it was still rather unnatural to witness. I had noticed that John never made a move to physically touch anyone if he could help it, me being the only exception. I still had yet to ascertain whether it was from a general aversion to physical affection, or merely a byproduct of his military standing and rank.

"Philip," John said hesitantly, and I noticed Edwards give an almost imperceptible nod in response. I knew caution was advised, though I thought this was perhaps a bit too extreme as there didn't seem to be anyone especially nearby.

Edwards drew even closer to our little group. "I've been sitting in the inn's lobby all day, eating and writing fake letters. I was hoping you would arrive today. Mr. West is still up in his room as far as I know. I can bring you there."

"What about the weapons and supplies? Any sign of the army?"

"No. To all of that, sir. The *only* thing I've found is Mr. West. He must be here for a reason, but I can't for the life of me tell what that reason is. I've made a thorough search of the nearby area too. It's *possible* I'm missing the items, but I feel like I've checked as many farms and storage areas as I can get away with. I'm beginning to think the letter to Eloise was either a hoax, or all of the items are long gone by now."

"Damn," John said, grinding a patch of dirt under his boot.

"So, should we go up there to try to get some answers out of Mr. West?" Edwards pressed.

John shot a quick look at me over his shoulder, his eyes creased and his lips pressed tight together. "Eloise," he said, "you stay with the horses."

"But I should go—" I began to protest at once.

"That's an order," he said sternly, his eyes no longer creased in thought, but narrowed in my direction.

I swallowed and shook my head silently, taking a step backward toward the horses.

He merely nodded to the other men and walked to the inn's front porch and stepped inside.

I knew I had to wait; there was nothing to be done. If Ben were upstairs, John and the other three would have him in no time. I briefly wondered if there were a back door to the building.

John was right, I thought then at once, when he said I shouldn't go into the inn with them. Perhaps John had been thinking of my feelings, and how hard this would be for me. Or he was simply considering the importance of keeping my whereabouts a secret for codebreaking purposes. Nevertheless, right as he was, this was torture.

My heart was racing, and I found myself pacing from horse to horse, petting them frantically and seeing nothing in front of my face. As the minutes passed, my stomach clenched. *What were they doing to him*, I wondered. I could envision him tied to a chair, blood streaming down his face as they demanded to know where the supplies had gone. Were they breaking his nose, his fingers? It scared me for a moment as I realized I didn't truly know what John was capable of when it came to matters of war. I had, up till now, only really seen him in times of safety, while he waited for the news that brought us to Darby. And now that it was here, it was too much. I could feel my stomach start to turn, and I prepared to lose my breakfast. Only by taking purposeful breaths did I manage to keep it in, though that didn't stop the ground from swirling beneath my feet.

Run, my mind suddenly commanded me. *You can't do this anymore.*

My own thoughts and impulses waged war with one another. *But what about John? What about Ben?*

I couldn't run, but I *would* go upstairs. I couldn't wait any longer. But what if I couldn't take what I found upstairs? Then what?

It didn't matter. I strode purposefully into the dark dining room at the front of the inn. Barely seeing where I was going, my eyes not yet adjusted to the dimness, I found the staircase at the back of the room and hurried up it. Seeing and hearing nothing but closed doors on the second floor, I continued up to the third. Still, there was nothing out of the ordinary.

Thinking of no better way to find my destination, I practically ran to the far door and knocked on it. There was no answer. I moved to the second, still no answer. I moved to the third. I was about to step away from it when it opened, and I found myself face-to-face with the barrel of a small gun.

I choked out a sort of yelp, like an injured dog, and passed out.

CHAPTER SIXTEEN

An Unexpected Communication

John was mad. His clenched fists and red face were the first things I saw as I came round.

"*What* are you doing here?" he yell-whispered at me. Edwards and the other two men stood uncomfortably in the corner. I slowly registered that they had laid me down on the room's bed.

"I—I panicked," I said, my mind foggy and words barely crossing the threshold into conscious thought.

"Panicked about what?" John asked. "Did something happen?" he followed up with, just a tad less anger in his voice.

"No. I...you were here for a long time."

"It's only been a few minutes!" John yell-whispered back.

"I—I'm sorry," I said, slowly sitting up and feeling a fresh wave of nausea wash over me. I swallowed hastily and looked down at my feet.

John sighed and ran a hand over his face. "I knew you shouldn't have come," he said. Sitting on the edge of the bed, he spoke to me quietly then, as the others moved even farther away and whispered amongst themselves. "This is hard on you because it's Ben, isn't it?" he asked, and this time I thought I detected genuine concern.

I nodded. "It's not that I still love him," I hastily explained.

"Perhaps not, but all of that doesn't always die quite

so easily I suppose," he said, laying a hand on my shoulder in an almost fatherly gesture. "Still," he said, and there was a blackness and intensity to his gaze as his eyes locked on mine, "you *need* to obey my orders next time. You could have compromised this whole thing."

"What..." I said, looking around the room again. "He's not here?"

"No, and we are going to wait in the room for a bit in case he comes right back. William thought you must have been him, which is why he pulled the gun on you. But why the hell William thought Ben would have knocked on his own door is beyond me."

"So..." I said, standing up slowly, feeling my way carefully toward a small desk, "are you sure he's still staying here?"

"Yes. Must have snuck out somehow. His drink was still warm even," John said, standing next to me and nodding toward the mug filled with a thick, black liquid. "And all his stuff is here," he said, nodding then toward a small pack and pile of clothes.

"No letters or anything?" I asked.

"Not that we found," he said.

"So I'm not even of use," I said quietly.

"Not right now, no. All you're managing to do is work yourself up into a panic."

I sighed and turned toward the window. John stepped behind me and laid a hand firmly on my shoulder as we looked out at the street below.

"What do we do now?"

"Wait around for Ben a little longer. Then Edwards will stay behind another day or two in case Ben comes back around. And we'll go on to Turnersville."

I spun around to face him. "You think the supplies might still be there?"

"Honestly, I'm not so sure," he said, and the creases around the corners of his eyes stood out strong. He grimaced in apparent discomfort. "We *cannot* lose those items if we're going to definitely pull off a campaign in the North, but...well, we have to at least check Turnersville. We have nothing else to go on just yet. Not unless we can find Ben after all."

He heaved a huge sigh and sat back down on the bed, his head cradled in his supporting palms.

Perhaps I should have gone to him, attempted to comfort him, but I found my eyes turning once more toward the street below. And for a split second, my brain told me that I had found Ben, down below. There were a bunch of people milling about the street, entering stores on this bright morning, but it was the back of one figure that turned the corner next to a tailor's shop that caught my eye. I couldn't have said whether it was the way he walked, his posture, or just the general shape of his body, but I instantly recognized it. Except then it was out of sight only a moment later. And so I began to doubt myself. How could I possibly know whether it was Ben after a split second staring at the back of a random man?

But if it had been Ben, did he see me in the window?

Another minute passed. "Are you all right? Did you see something?" I spun around, my eyes wide, as John stepped over to me.

"No. At least, I don't think so," I said.

"You were staring outside with this intense gaze," John said, standing near me now and surveying the street below as well.

"It's just...I thought I saw him at first, but now I'm not so sure."

"Where?" John asked.

"Near the tailor's," I answered.

"Edwards, with me," he said at once, marching toward the door. "Eloise, stay here and identify Ben if he comes to the room."

And John was gone, visible in the street less than a minute later. I watched from the window as John and Edwards strode with purpose into the tailor's stop. I knew Ben wasn't *in* the tailor's shop, but there was certainly no correcting John from up in the inn.

And yet two whole minutes passed before John and Edwards came back out, looking around them, but no longer with that unwavering focus they had before. Slowly, cautiously, they walked around the building, coming back out to the main street a moment later. John conferred with Edwards very briefly before they looked up at the window where I stood. John gave me a searching look and shrug of a shoulder. I shook my head no, I hadn't seen him again. John shook his head once and motioned for me to come to him.

"He wants us down there," I said.

"All of us?" William asked.

"I guess we'll know for sure when we talk to him," I said, marching past William and out into the tight hallway.

Outside, William and the other soldier, Harold, in tow, I talked with John in the middle of the street.

"No sign of him, but he certainly saw *you*," John said grimly, his lips making a tight line, his eyes narrowed at me.

"How can you be sure it was him? And that he saw me?" I asked. I was afraid at this point—afraid that John wouldn't want me anymore because I was useless to him as a spy, afraid to hear how John knew Ben had seen me in the first place, even afraid to hear what Ben thought of me.

Then, only as he held it out to me, did I realize John was holding a small note, simply folded in half.

"The man in the store said he was expecting some people of our description, and that a fellow had left a note for him to give us," John said, withdrawing the note from my reach just as I put my hand out to take it.

"But you didn't find Ben?" I asked. I was trembling all over; after all, none of my questions had yet been answered.

"I walked around the store just in case, but he clearly has a hiding place or had already been able to make his escape if he were brazen enough to have left this. Still...William, Edwards, I want the two of you to remain here indefinitely. Send word to Turnersville if you find him, and I'll of course reach out to you here if needed. I want you to turn this town upside down looking for him. Keep your ears open for news of his departure. I want to know *everything* that has to do with Benjamin West. Finding him may be the only way of actually recovering those supplies, and I will *not* report to the lieutenant colonel that we have failed. Do you understand me?"

"Yes, sir," William said.

"If he's here, we'll find him," Edwards added.

"Right," John said. "Come on, Harold. Eloise," he said, walking toward our horses.

Touching my horse's nose softly, I looked briefly into his big, dark eyes. "John?" I asked, gathering my courage. John looked at me, his features stoic and immovable. "What did the note say?"

"That's none of your concern for now. I'll show you back at camp. In the meantime, I'd like to get out of this town. The tailor *seemed* ignorant of our identities and purpose, but that doesn't mean he actually is," he said, and he swung onto his horse and already started away as I followed.

I looked back at William and Edwards one more time as my horse moved forward. They were again walking down the small space between the tailor's and the house next door. I wondered how much danger they were being put in by staying.

CHAPTER SEVENTEEN

The Next Steps

The woods were beautiful. The shade kept it cool, and the sunlight streamed in through golden patches. My horse's hooves crunched through a perpetual layer of dead leaves as we made it to the small clearing where John, I, and three other soldiers had set up camp. The rest were spread out amongst a rather large amount of space. In the days preceding our arrival at Darby, we had travelled in small groups, using messengers between the groups to facilitate planned stops and routes, all in an attempt to call as little attention to ourselves as possible.

Although I was still nervous for a variety of reasons, I had managed to talk myself into a semi-state of calm. After all, John truly believed Ben wasn't within our grasp, or I wouldn't have believed he would leave. And my continued presence with him seemed to indicate that he did not intend on doing away with me. Still, I couldn't be one hundred percent certain.

As we moved off our horses and offered them a drink, John kept his gaze carefully diverted from my own. The letter was not visible, but I was still dying to know what it said. After watering the horses, John walked toward his tent, throwing off his coat and unbuttoning the collar at the neck. And then he simply stood there in the opening of his tent, staring at the ground in front of him.

I walked to my own tent, but remained outside, watching

him, wondering what he was doing, just waiting.

After a few minutes, I couldn't take it anymore. Throwing off the straw hat, I marched up to him. "I need to know," I said, stronger than I had intended.

John looked up at me slowly, his face almost expressionless save for a minor twitch at the corner of his mouth. "You need to know what?" he asked.

"I need to know if you plan on ridding yourself of me at this point."

Whatever John had been expecting, it clearly wasn't that. His mouth had opened slightly and his eyes had gone round like an owl's. "What? What on earth do you mean?"

"I'm no good to you as a sort of spy any longer," I said, trying to still my shaking hands by clenching the sides of my skirt. "So you have no reason to keep me around."

"Is...is *that* what you're afraid of?" he asked, and it was as if his entire exterior were melting as I watched all of the tension drain from his shoulders. Without warning, he reached forward then and embraced me. It took me a moment to realize I was being hugged and not pushed away, and thus a moment for me to reach up and hug him back.

"I'm not doing away with you," he said down into my hair. "I can't believe that's what you were afraid of. I...I love you," he said, and I shook against him.

"I love you too," I echoed.

Giving me a quick, tighter squeeze he released me and looked down into my eyes. "I figure you'd like to see the note too at this point," he said, handing it to me.

I opened it as John came around to reread it over my shoulder.

I don't know who you are, but I know this is the beginning of the end for you. I promise you that you'll be dead soon. No one can expect to simply kidnap Eloise. I saw you in the window next to Eloise. I didn't recognize you. But that doesn't mean you aren't kidnapping her as a way to get to me, or simply because you expect money from me, one or the other. Either way, you picked the wrong man to attack, unfortunately.

You can wait up in my room as long as you like, indeed. But I will come for you when you're not expecting me now. You've tipped your hand, and I will rescue Eloise from you thugs. But I promise you, you are looking at an end most unfortunate. In the end, my punishment will find you most remorseful.

There is, perhaps, only one thing that can save you now. Release Eloise. Don't bother running. There is no place on earth that will keep you safe. To me, Eloise is valuable. To you, she spells out your doom, and imminently.

As soon as you read this, you should release her and leave. It is your ONLY chance to still live. If not, your death will be long and excruciating.

Ben

I swallowed once, hard, and looked up at John, though he was smiling, a surprisingly toothy grin. "You see? Your cover hasn't been blown at all! In fact, he thinks you're in *danger*." John laughed lightly then. "I'll tell you what," he said, still chuckling as he refolded the paper and shoved it in his coat pocket once more, "he may be a code breaker, but he's not that smart. Either that, or he's blinded by misplaced love."

I stayed silent on the topic, allowing John to have his moment of triumph. "Well, I'm glad I didn't mess things up," I eventually added.

"Not at all. If anything, this actually might be a *good* thing. I was thinking about that on the way back to the camp. You see, if he's distracted with trying to free you from kidnappers, he won't be any trouble while we try to figure out what happened to those supplies. We'll start in Turnersville, and if everything is really gone, we just might be able to use you as bait. So you see, you're not useless at all! You may be the key to us getting exactly what we need to win this war!"

I sighed and leaned against his chest. "I hope so."

I didn't see John for most of the day after that. He went off riding through the woods to let the men know the next step in the plan.

One of the men in our camp had managed to shoot some birds, and so I busied myself with cleaning and cooking them in the late afternoon. By the time John returned to the camp, they were a crispy, golden brown, and they smelled delicious.

"See! Even more reasons why you are useful," he joked, jabbing playfully at my ribs. I laughed and fixed him a plate, tucking a strand of my chestnut hair behind my ear as sweat dribbled down the sides of my temples. It wasn't particularly hot under the trees, but working over the open fire had changed that pretty quickly.

"Well," John said, sitting cross-legged on a patch of leaves, setting his plate on his lap, "we're all set to leave for Turnersville tomorrow."

"How long will it take?"

"At least a couple of days. We'll have to be careful. We're not exactly in friendly territory, and we don't really know what's waiting for us there. With Darby being so empty, I can't help but wonder if the real trap is in Turnersville."

"I agree," I said.

"Yes. Or...the trap was in Darby, but your letter called it off, as it seemed that everything was okay. To be honest, I'm really starting to think that the letter Ben sent you about the weapons being moved was *meant* to fall into our hands."

I stopped fixing my own plate, and turned to look at him as he continued to explain.

"What if it was all a ruse to get us into Darby? If so, we played it well, staying spread out and hidden. But there still didn't seem to be any sign of a trap. Maybe we took too long traveling here, and they gave up. We may never know, but my *hope*, in that case, is that the weapons and supplies and men are still in Turnersville."

I finished cutting my own slice of bird, and came to sit next to John on the ground. "Well, we can hope."

CHAPTER EIGHTEEN

Ben's Friends in Miston

W e were leading the soldiers, although we didn't often lay eyes on them the next couple of days. We tried to keep mostly to thick patches of trees when possible, avoiding towns altogether. There were some open fields we risked crossing, but even then we tried to stay on the outskirts. The sun was setting on our second day of traveling, and the heat was not dissipating nearly as much as I had hoped as the day drew to a close. "It's going to be a hot one tomorrow," John said, raising his hand to shield his eyes against the setting sun.

"Well, it's just about June now, right?"

"Just about," John agreed.

A town had sprung up on the horizon, and as we walked toward it, it appeared to be on the larger side. "That's not Turnersville, is it?" I asked.

"Only one way to find out," he said, and he instructed the men traveling with us to hang back and retreat into the woods to find a safe place to camp for the night, and to let the other groups know we would be stopping here. "Eloise and I will head into the town, try to figure out where we are."

As they left, I looked at John, his skin already tanning from the long days of traveling north. "It feels almost strange to be alone," I commented, keeping my eyes firmly focused on the town before us. "We've had the company of your soldiers for so long."

"It is," he said, and I could feel the weight of his eyes shift to my face. "Though not an unwelcome change, I hope?"

I turned and faced him as my horse continued straight and steadfast. "Oh, not at all. Just unusual, you know?"

He smirked and tilted his head, eyeing the town once more. "I might be convinced to stay the night in an inn in the town, you know. If you'd like a brief lifestyle change."

"Oh! I could have an actual bed?" I asked, thinking of the rather firm, and by now uncomfortable, cot I had been afforded, which in and of itself was a luxury on this trip, one that not all of the men with us had.

"Yes," John said lightly. "We could have an actual bed."

I turned my head sharply toward him, but he was merely looking ahead at the town, a rather determined expression on his face, his normally pale blue eyes blazing like fire in the sunlight.

As we reached the buildings on the edge of the town, John greeted a few townspeople cordially, getting hat lifts and "good afternoons" in response. One particularly genial man, who had greeted John with a full "good afternoon, my fine sir," must have piqued John's interest enough.

"Would you mind telling us which town we've made it to?" John asked in a surprisingly convincing northern accent.

"This here is Miston, sir."

"Miston. Hm. We were trying to make it to Turnersville."

"Oh, well, you're not too terribly far off. Should probably make it there tomorrow, I would say. Just keep heading west."

"Thank you. Good to know we're not horribly lost," John said.

"Where you coming from?" the gentleman asked, rubbing his hand absentmindedly over his stomach as if already anticipating his dinner.

The catch in John's breath was nearly imperceptible, but just enough for me to step in with confidence.

"Moorestown, sir. New Jersey," I spoke up.

"You're fairly far from home then," he said. "Visiting family?"

"Yes. We're newly married, and we're going to visit my wife's family," John said, gesturing toward me.

"Well, congratulations to the two of you then," he said with a large smile, showing a couple of missing teeth.

"Could you point us in the direction of the inn?" John asked, and my stomach twisted in nervousness.

"Yes, sir. It's that tall building sticking up here, you see it? On this side of the street," he said, gesturing to a structure only a minute away.

"Yes, I do. Thank you for the information."

"You're very welcome," he said, and he tipped his hat to us again as we pushed our horses onward at a slow trot.

"Won't the men miss us?" I asked.

"I can head back in a bit, tell them not to expect us tonight," John said with a shrug of his shoulders. "I'm glad to hear we're not far off, even if this isn't Turnersville."

"Yes," I agreed, my mind elsewhere.

As we drew up to the inn, John practically jumped from his horse, motioning for me to do the same. "Well, this seems to be a nice, respectable-looking establishment," he said, nodding his head in approval as he assessed the building's facade.

"It is," a couple of men in dark blue uniforms said behind us, still perched on their own horses.

John turned and his look of pure bliss disappeared, though he quickly repainted a cordial smile upon his face.

"Glad to hear it, sirs. I'm traveling in these parts with my wife, Maggie," he said with a nod toward me.

I gave a brief curtsy, still clutching my horse's reins with the one hand.

"I see. And your name is?"

"Dan Jones," he said at once.

"Ah. And what brings you to Miston, Mr. and Mrs. Jones?"

"We're headed to Turnersville to visit my wife's family," he said.

"Turnersville, huh? Bit of a volatile area from what I hear. A few mischief-makers in that area."

"I can assure you my wife's family are not in that category," John said, his face worked into creased lines around his eyes and an engaging, inviting smile on his lips.

"Good to hear," one of the men on the horses said. "Well, I'm sorry to bother you, but perhaps we might ask you a few questions. Being as you're travelers."

"Of course," John said. "Should we go into the inn?"

"Oh, I think the alley should be fine. Off the beaten track enough to give us some privacy. We won't be long," the man assured us. I saw John's shoulder twitch.

"Let's just tie up our horses and step over there," the soldier added, and he nodded to his partner who also dismounted and walked with us to the side of the inn where we could put our horses.

"You're soldiers, I see," John said, eyeing the uniforms, clean and pressed.

"Yes, and that's why you might be able to help us," the more vocal of the two responded. He wasn't much older than me, I noticed, with light brown hair, green eyes, and a face full of freckles. The other had a much darker complexion, with deep, almost dangerous eyes that looked at us suspiciously.

John followed the soldiers toward the alley on the other side of the building, adjusting his coat as he walked, and I saw him move his hand casually toward the opening of his jacket on the right side. I tensed immediately; he kept his gun there.

As soon as the shadows pressed upon us, the freckled soldier turned abruptly, thankfully finding John assuming a more or less normal stance, aside from his right hand positioned near his hip. "So," the soldier said, "we're looking for a friend of ours. Last seen in Darby."

"Darby?" John asked, his eyebrows the only part of him noticeably moving.

"Yes. Have you been there?"

"Like I said, we're traveling to see my wife's family, but

I don't think we went through Darby. Did we, honey?" he said, turning toward me.

"It was in the distance, but we didn't stop at the town," I replied, trying my best to guess at John's intentions.

"Ah, okay. We're looking for a young lady to be precise. Kidnapped by someone. Goes by the name of Eloise," the darker soldier said sternly.

I saw John's hand twitch at the side of his coat again, and I choked on my own air, causing an absurd coughing fit as all three men turned to stare at me.

"Are you all right?" John asked, placing his hand tenderly on my back.

"Fine, fine," I said, waving him off. "Just a tickle in my throat. Probably all of the dust," I said with a flip of my hand, indicating the roads around us. I recovered myself and stood up tall once more. "I'm sorry. You were saying?" I directed my question at the soldiers.

"We are looking for a kidnapped young lady who goes by the name of Eloise," the darker soldier continued, looking at me directly.

"That's a shame, but we haven't seen or heard of any ladies in distress," John said. "Now, if you'll excuse me, I'd like to go check in to the inn with my wife," he said, laying a hand on my elbow, purposefully turning me with the motion.

"Just a moment, if you please," the freckled man spoke up once more. "We'd like to speak to your *wife*, sir. In private."

I saw the muscles in John's jaw snap tightly against his face, his right hand immediately moving from my elbow to his right side once more. A quick glance at the soldiers' stances told me they were far from relaxed as well. My breath caught in my chest.

"That won't be necessary," John said, his voice dark and measured. "Anything you have to say to my wife, you can say in front of me. Questioning my *wife* without me present is most unusual, I'm sure."

"We were just hoping to have a word with her, a lady's

intuition being what it is. Perhaps she noticed something," the freckled man said, his voice even, yet not entirely unfriendly.

I sensed John's right arm twitch again, and I knew that things were about to go very, very poorly.

"It's okay, really," I said, taking a step forward, almost between the men in an impulsive act of either sheer bravery or stupidity. "I have nothing to hide that my husband can't hear. My name is Maggie Jones, not Eloise if that's what you're implying."

"How do we know you're not simply saying that under duress?" the man with the penetrating eyes asked, or more threatened.

John's whole posture shifted, and I knew I had a matter of seconds before weapons were drawn. "I can assure you," I said loudly, purposefully turning toward the soldiers and away from John lest I appear panicked by his movement. "I *swear* on my Aunt Bessie's grave in New York I'm safe."

The freckled man's eyes widened. "No need to swear, Mrs. Jones. We believe you," he said, and I felt the tenseness seep out of the alley. I heard John shift his weight behind me, and I took a discreet breath of air into my burning lungs.

"I do apologize to you both. We can't be too sure about travelers during these uncertain times," the soldier continued. "Now, would you care to be staying in our fine inn for the night?" he asked.

I turned and saw John open his mouth to speak, but I cut him off. "I for one am exhausted, though I am looking forward to seeing my family in Turnersville as soon as possible. We're going to be seeing my parents and brothers, and my other Aunt Bessie, who recently moved in with my parents but originally lived closer to us in New Jersey. The inn will be a welcome rest. And then when we reach my family tomorrow, it should be a fun event, and they'll get to see Dan, whom they've only met once before," I rambled.

The freckled man cocked his head at me, almost as if he were unsure. "Very well. Enjoy the inn," he said, and they walked past us back onto the brighter main street.

As soon as they were out of sight, John leaned against the side of the building and wiped the hair away from his forehead. His forehead glistened even in the shadows, and I realized the full extent of his nervousness then.

"There were two of them and one of me," he said. "And who knows how many townspeople would have been on us had we begun firing shots," he said quietly, staring up at the strip of sky above the building.

I stepped over to him and laid my hand on his chest. "It's all right," I said.

He covered my hand with his own and turned his head down to smile at me. "I suppose it is. You were wonderful. Very convincing."

I smiled shyly.

"How about we get something to eat then and ask about a room?" he said, taking my hand and leading me toward the busy street. I looked about us, and while I saw several groups of people talking, entering shops, and walking, I did not see the two soldiers. John led the way into the inn, where we stepped into a nearly empty dining room at the front with a small desk area off to the left side. John strode purposefully in that direction.

"Hello. Do you have a room available for the night, for me and my wife?" he asked.

"Of course, sir," the man answered, and I turned around to scan the dining room, focusing on the lone customer in the corner reading a newspaper. I saw his foot shift, but the newspaper remained up, covering his face.

"Are you all right?" I heard John's voice, practically in my ear.

"Oh! Yes, sorry," I responded still quietly, but with a small jump. John must have noticed for he followed my gaze toward the man in the corner. I felt him stiffen again next to me. The man at the desk was still talking genially, and I saw John pull out some money from his jacket, though I also saw him keep his right hand once more poised and ready to withdraw more dangerous items from within it. While he didn't turn around again, I noticed his peripheral vision was set on me, and I did my best to look ahead and not direct my attention to the hidden man with the newspaper.

"And we'd like to have a bite to eat first, if you don't mind," John was saying.

"Naturally, naturally," the man at the desk said. "Take a seat wherever you'd like, and Marie will be out to serve you momentarily."

John turned then and strode slowly, quietly toward a table along the back wall, somewhat close to the man with the newspaper. He pulled out a seat for me where I would be facing away from the man, and I necessarily sat in it. John chose the seat across from me. He slowly pulled out his gun, I saw, and held it hidden beneath the table.

"Who is it?" I mouthed silently, though John ignored my question, focusing instead on the man.

"Oh good! You're still here!" a rather loud voice sliced through the still air of the inn's dining room, and I was extremely surprised to see the two soldiers walk in, striding purposefully toward our table. John's head appeared to be on a swivel then, from the soldiers back to the man behind the newspaper. Though as he looked in the mystery man's direction, I saw his brows furrow together, and I couldn't help but turn to face the source of his confusion. The man had lowered his newspaper for a moment to take in the new arrivals walking toward our table. And I was equally as shocked to see a complete stranger sitting there. His dark gray hair and finely trimmed mustache situated between exceedingly red and puffy cheeks bore absolutely no resemblance to the young man I had feared was hiding at that table. I instead switched my attention to the soldiers, only then remembering that John's gun was already drawn and situated discreetly under the table.

The soldiers either had no idea how close they were to danger or believed their message would hardly warrant any violence as the freckled man spoke in a friendly manner. "I just wanted to apologize again for our demeanor earlier. Like I said before, you never can be too careful these days. However, I wanted to let you both know that I actually heard from another traveler just now that there are some suspicious individuals camping in the woods nearby. We're going to give some of our friends another hour to get here from the next town over, and we're going to investigate. With any luck, we'll have rescued Eloise Brown before midnight tonight. So again, so sorry to have bothered you fine people." And with a touch of the brim of his hat, the two strode outside.

I looked over at John who had sat in sullen silence throughout the entire interaction. Our eyes locked, and I saw his shoulders move heavily. "Well, I suppose we won't be able to spend the night here after all," he said very lowly.

"No," I said, my volume matching his, though perhaps not the gravity. "I suppose we can't."

He rose then and walked to the innkeeper. "I am extremely sorry for the inconvenience, sir," he told the desk clerk, "but we just heard news about some kidnappers in the area. My wife no longer feels safe and wishes to travel on, at least to the next town."

"Kidnappers?" the man asked, shocked eyes wide on his pale face. "Well then wouldn't you be safer here in the inn than out on the open road?"

"I would think so, but my wife is insistent."

"Ah," he said, eyeing me quite critically. "Very well then," he said, opening a drawer and counting out some money, which he slowly slid to John.

"Thank you. And again, I am very sorry for the inconvenience," John repeated.

Outside, the soldiers were once again out of sight, despite their horses being still tied next to ours. John took that in and whispered to me, close enough I could feel his hot breath on my face. "We'll have to hurry. Leaving will look suspicious, but staying could doom the men and, more importantly, the mission."

I nodded, climbed atop my horse with John's help, and in a

matter of minutes, we were racing for the trees.

CHAPTER NINETEEN

Welcome to Turnersville

By noon the next day, we were all exhausted. John declared that we needed to stop, at least for a couple hours. Trekking through the night after a full day of travel was no joke, and after sending one of the men back to relay the message to the next group, hopefully causing a ripple effect, John practically slid from his horse. He barely fed and tied the horses to a nearby tree before curling into a pile of leaves, tipping his hat over his eyes. I followed suit, finding some pine needles beneath a tree slick with sap where I lay down and closed my own eyes.

Despite the exhaustion, I found that sleep eluded me at first. I had, after all, remained straight as a beanpole all night, on high alert as I waited anxiously for the sound of gunfire to ring out from the forest as a group of our men would surely come in contact with the soldiers or their reinforcements. But none came, and no news reached us of any sort of confrontation. Poor Eli Richardson, a soldier traveling in the middle of the pack, spent a rather exhausting night hopping from group to group, checking on everyone and making sure that we were all together and safe.

It was finally at that point, on the verge of sleep, that my brain caught up with my fears. And I wondered if anyone had been coming for us at all.

I dreamt then. John was kissing me in it, and while he was

doing so, he turned into a snake. A big one. He lunged for me and wrapped around my body, squeezing so tight I could barely breathe. I was gasping for air, coughing as I couldn't fill my chest.

"Eloise," I heard the whisper and felt the hand on my shoulder. I jumped even as I was aware I was no longer sleeping. John was looking down at me, concern evident in the creases around his eyes, even in the quickly gathering darkness. "Are you all right? You started coughing in your sleep."

"Oh, I'm fine. I was just having a bad dream," I said sheepishly. I turned and looked toward the edge of the woods where I saw that the sunlight was all but gone.

There was a pause while I continued looking out toward the edge of the forest and the field barely visible beyond. Then, finally, "Was it a bad dream about me?" he asked.

"What?" I said, snapping my neck back to look at him.

He smirked at me, and I felt a ball of guilt in my stomach. "You're hesitant to make eye contact," he observed.

I sighed. "I dreamt that we were…kissing," I said, feeling my cheeks burn bright red, and I saw the hint of a smile pass across John's lips. "But then you turned into a snake and started strangling me," I said, attempting to convey an apology with my grimace.

John's eyebrows shot up. "Well, my mother always told me that our dreams aren't some magic crystal ball into the future, but simply a mix of everything we've been dealing with. Do you want my guess as to why you dreamt that?" he asked, turning and sitting next to me in the pine needles. I nodded. "I think—at least I *hope*—that you enjoy kissing me. And you were, perhaps, looking forward to doing so. But then the whole situation in Miston turned sour and scary, and that's why you dreamt about the snake part."

I sighed deeply and rested my head against his shoulder. "Thank you," I said quietly.

He kissed the top of my head.

"Come on now," he said, standing and offering me a hand

up off the ground. "Now that we've gotten a bit of rest, the plan is to eat a little something and travel through the night again. We can't be that far from Turnersville at this point. Are you good using the cornmeal we brought to cook with?" he asked. I nodded and set to work.

Even though we had been stopped for a long while by the time we set out again in the deep darkness, I was immediately fatigued as I sat in the saddle. I was sick of traveling, sick of being surrounded by soldiers, sick of feeling like my love life was always on the brink of disaster. I wanted rest, and I wanted to feel safe and secure. But the war didn't care about rest, sucking it up like a tornado instead, thriving on fear and sleeplessness. I hoped, not for the first time, that what I was doing would actually make a difference. That my actions could help end the war, and bring more loving brothers like Ethan home to their families.

I had to believe that, and that thought kept me in the saddle as we rode toward Turnersville.

The sky was barely lightening when we saw a farmstead in front of us, out through the thinning trees. "I'll go check on it," Harold Lemper said, and with a nod of consent from John, he urged his horse out of the trees, toward the farm as the rest of us pulled our horses to a stop. I could barely see him reach the farm as I heard the cry of a rooster. He was out of sight for only a few minutes when I saw him returning on his horse. But then his one horse seemed to turn into two as I realized he wasn't alone.

"Is this all right?" I turned and asked John, who had tensed up. "It's not if they've got Harold and we've got company," he said sternly. But after another minute, I was able to recognize Harold's black and tan horse, and soon after, Harold himself. I saw John relax and move his hand away from his holstered gun.

"We've made it!" Harold called once he was within shouting distance, and I then noticed the huge grin plastered across his face.

As they drew up to us, I took in his companion, a man, perhaps in his early forties, with a grizzled gray and brown beard and the darkest eyes I had ever seen. He tipped his hat at us, and in a rather husky voice boomed out, "Welcome to Turnersville, my fine gentlemen."

"Thank you kindly," John said with a nod of his head. "You're...expecting us?" he asked slowly and uncertainly, his eyes darting back and forth between the farmer and Harold.

"Of course, Captain," the man responded. "And I think you'll be quite pleased with the gifts we have for you. Are you ready to go?"

John's eyebrows shot up. "Of course, of course," he agreed hastily, and the man slowly turned his horse on a trajectory somewhat overshooting the nearby farmhouse.

"I'll tell the others," Harold volunteered, and he was off like a rabbit into the trees.

It was just me, John, and two other soldiers then, aside from the newcomer who immediately made to introduce himself as soon as John urged his horse next to him. "Name's Caleb Jordan," he said as I fell into place behind his and John's horses.

"Captain Cardis," John said seriously.

"Well, it is a pleasure to meet you, sir," Mr. Jordan said. "We were beginning to think you were never going to make it. Though rumors do reach this part of our state, and we thought that if we were going to see you, the time would be soon. You'll want to be prepared, I know, for any coming battles in this area of the world. And a campaign in hostile territory will not be easy, I know."

"Indeed," John said.

"It's a small town, but we have I guess what you could call a main street through the trees that way," he said with a nod of his head past the farm. "Still a bit of a distance, to be honest. We're fairly secluded out here. Now, we're heading to the next farm over. You'll find quite the welcoming committee there.

We've had over a hundred fighting men here for almost a month now. And that's not to mention the rather impressive arsenal we've gathered, if I do say so myself."

John's eyes widened. "We had received information that you and your supplies had been captured and moved to Darby."

At this Mr. Jordan laughed loudly. "Captured? You need to find yourself some more accurate information. It's true that some people have come snooping around here. It's not easy to hide a hundred-some men, after all! But we've made it through just fine. Never come close to *anything* like an official run-in with soldiers or anything. And they're not in these parts anyway."

"Mm," John said, turning his head so that he was almost able to look at me. It was clear, at this point, that the correspondence from Ben mentioning Darby was misleading at best.

The next farm over was not terribly far away, and we were headed straight toward the rather oversized barn. As we neared it, Mr. Jordan let out something akin to a whoop and two men quickly appeared around the corner of the elongated barn. "They're here!" Mr. Jordan cried out, taking off his hat and waving it back and forth above his head as we trotted the last paces to the barn.

Dozens of men started trickling out from it, and we were quickly swarmed by clean, eager faces beaming up at us, outstretched hands ready to shake John's and shouted greetings ranging from "About time!" to "Welcome to the friendliest territory in the North!"

"Back everyone! Give the captain some air!" Mr. Jordan hollered happily over the crowd.

After a minute or two, the men naturally backed off, allowing the other couple soldiers, Mr. Jordan, and John and I to come down from our horses.

"Captain Cardis," Mr. Jordan said as a man approached us, "may I introduce Captain Connoway? Once a Union officer, Captain Connoway has come to realize the foolishness of the Union, and has decided to switch sides." Captain Connoway stepped forward and actually saluted John who, a bit startled, nevertheless saluted in response.

Captain Connoway had the brightest blond hair I had ever seen, almost white, although he was clearly very young, with almost porcelain skin. After he had lowered his hand, he casually said, "Obviously I have no illusions of keeping my officer's rank, though the men here have sort of rallied around me as I have the most military experience," he said, a sideways smirk on his thin lips. "Name's Daniel Connoway, and while we don't have the most battle-hardened men here, I think you'll find that all are in exceptional shape, and have been drilled by me in anticipation of your arrival."

John and I looked past Daniel Connoway at this point and surveyed the men before us. Indeed, they were young and trim, rather eager expressions on their faces, and had they been in uniforms, I would have believed in an instant that every one of them were prepared for war.

John nodded, a smile playing over his lips. "I thank you, Mr. Connoway. I can't wait to assess them. And we, of course, thank you all for the much needed supplies."

"Well, we had quite a few connections in that respect," Daniel Connoway responded, nodding in a couple different directions at the crowd. "Men with the know-how and resources to get the job done. Though hiding those resources from the Union was no joke, as you might imagine."

"Of course," John said with a nod of his head.

"Now, I expect you'll be tired from your journey," Mr. Jordan piped back up. "We'll make sure you and your men are well fed and rested. We'll be waiting for news from your higher-ups, or do you have immediate plans to mobilize us?" he continued.

At the phrase "higher-ups," I saw John's shoulders tense ever so briefly before almost imperceptibly shaking it off. "I will want to report to my lieutenant colonel, but really only to confirm that we acquired the supplies and troops and see where he would like them. Though, assuming there hasn't been a wild change of plans, my latest reports indicate that the army will be attempting to take the North once and for all in the near future. We may not be so far from the fighting as you might think," John said proudly, standing up to his full, impressive height.

"Very good," Captain Connoway said. "Shall I give you a little tour then while the rest of your men trickle in?" he asked with a nod over John's shoulder. I turned and saw the first little cluster of our soldiers almost arrived at our location.

"Certainly. Thank you," John said, and without being invited, I glued myself to his side, eager to see what was so important that it necessitated all of this fuss and planning.

Turning in at the barn entrance, it took a moment for my eyes to adjust to the faded light, but once they did, I was shocked at the number of crates and barrels before me.

"Now, I know you gentlemen would do just fine without us, I'm sure, but given that you're going to attempt this important push up here, our hope is that these might help give you the advantage, push your victory over the edge," Captain Connoway said, prying the lid off of a nearby crate.

John's eyebrows rose, illuminated in a patch of light through the slats of the barn. "Repeating arms," he said with a nod of his head.

"And don't you worry about the ammunition, Captain," Captain Connoway said at once. "We've seen to collecting a rather solid supply. We've been at this for quite a while, you see, and more than one of those volunteers outside were perfectly positioned for purchasing and constructing these items."

"You believe these will be able to be used freely in the coming campaign?" John asked.

Captain Connoway laughed just slightly. "Captain, our advertisements were not false, I assure you."

John smiled, showing his teeth. "Well, I think this trip has been well worth it then."

"I didn't even show you the ammunition yet," Captain Connoway said proudly. "Some of the most reliable stuff. And for good measure, we've got some of the finest canons money can buy. In another barn, of course. Oh! And over here," he said, quickly opening another crate, "breech-loading weapons, and a boatload of them!"

"Well," John said, looking around the barn, "I'm impressed."

"We haven't even finished the tour! There are still two more barns nearby."

CHAPTER TWENTY

The Dance

A mutual acquaintance of our families had brought both Ben and me to a rather impressive estate on the outskirts of Philadelphia only the day after my sixteenth birthday. And while I knew the party they were throwing was not for me, it had felt, to me, almost like my own party, a chance to celebrate growing up with my fanciest dress and lots of people to talk to.

The old house had an ornate ballroom, with fancy trim work of golden swirls around the edges of the ceiling. I could have spent all day in that room, staring at it above thick maroon curtains framing windows that looked out onto an expansive lawn. I remember I was looking at it when suddenly two hands came from behind me and covered my eyes. "Guess who," the familiar voice said.

I immediately reached up and slid the hands from my eyes, spinning around a bit angrier than I felt. "Ben," I scolded, "stop that. People will think we're only children, acting that way."

"Nonsense," Ben said, crossing his arms in front of him. "I see my father play that way with my mother all the time, and he's quite old as fathers come."

"Still," I insisted, hiding any smile.

Ben furrowed his dark brows. "Why so grumpy?" he asked.

"I'm not grumpy," I insisted, albeit feeling my mood begin to match my demeanor. "I simply want to enjoy this event as a woman and not a child. It's not every day we're invited to parties like this one."

Ben heaved a deep sigh. "Very well," he said, his head no longer sitting confidently above his shoulders, but rather defeated with a slight downward look.

I was on the verge of apologizing—after all, it was a big night for Ben too—when my eyes locked with a young man quite a few steps behind him. The young man smiled at me, and I smiled shyly back. The room was packed with people at this point, and the musicians were playing loudly as dancers filled the center of the room, but the young man began making his way toward me, undeterred. His hair was black like the night, yet his skin was the color of milk. He was more like a portrait than a real person.

It was only as the man was almost to us did I realize Ben had been speaking. "What was that?" I asked.

"I said there are quite a lot of people dancing," Ben said, his green eyes shining in the lantern light.

"Hello there," the man cut in. "I don't believe we've met," he said, looking only at me. "I'm Gabriel Press. I live practically next door to Mr. Drammond," he added, referencing our host.

"Eloise Brown," I said with a bow of my head.

"Benjamin West," Ben said, his eyes squinted sharply at the new arrival.

"Pleasure," he said to us, though with only the briefest of glances at Ben. "Would you care to dance, Miss Brown?"

"Certainly," I said, my chest, neck, and face tingling in nervous excitement.

Stepping onto the dance floor, Gabriel took my hand in one of his and my waist with the other. While I hadn't truly had the chance to dance at any large gatherings prior to this one, my mother had made sure I knew all of the popular dances of the day. And Gabriel was a fine dance partner. "You're a very good dancer," he whispered, though I knew I was passable at best. I merely smiled at him.

"You look lovely in that shade of blue, by the way," he continued. "It makes your dark eyes shine."

"Thank you," I said with the briefest of glances at my deep blue dress with white edges. "You look very nice yourself," I said, motioning toward his black and white suit.

"Thank you," he said with a quick smile that flashed shockingly white teeth.

After the dance was over, he made a slight bow and asked if he could find me a drink.

"Thank you," I accepted.

"Where are you from?" he asked as we made our way to the edge of the dance floor and thus the other party-goers milling thickly about the edges.

"Not too terribly far. New Jersey in—" but I stopped talking as Ben strode up to me purposefully, tall glass in hand.

"Eloise, I got you a drink. I thought you may be thirsty."

"Oh!" I said, my hand wavering indecisively in front of me. I shot a panicked look at Gabriel, though he was looking in Ben's direction. I turned to follow his gaze just in time to see Ben staring hard and directly at Gabriel.

Gabriel cleared his throat. "Seeing as you've already been brought something to drink, I'll take a brief leave of you, though I do hope to talk to you again before the night is through," he said, taking my hand briefly, shooting an indeterminate look at Ben, and departing.

As soon as I hoped Gabriel was out of earshot, I let Ben have it. "What are you doing?" I practically spat at him.

"I brought you a drink," he said, holding it out once more.

"Don't be stupid, Benjamin," I said again. "You were trying to scare off Gabriel."

"That man is way too old for you," he said, spastically shoving his hand in the general direction of Gabriel's departure.

"He is *not*," I insisted, and truly I didn't believe Gabriel to be more than a few years older than me.

"Well, then," Ben said, his eyes narrowing, "what kind

of a man steps in between another man and woman who are clearly talking, and interrupts and takes the woman away?" I momentarily registered that he had referred to us as a man and woman, but quickly shoved that thought down as I continued to argue with him.

"He asked me to dance. He didn't stab you and carry me away on a horse like the plunders of war," I said icily, aware of others around us and trying not to call attention to ourselves over the din of the party.

"Well, it's not right. I didn't even get the chance to ask you to dance myself."

"Would you have even asked?"

"What do you mean by that?" Ben countered.

"Sometimes I swear that you're afraid to talk to me," I said, coming up with stuff I didn't even know was in my brain in the first place. "You send me all of these codes, but never say anything at all...*intimate* in real life."

"That's not true at all," Ben responded, eyes wide. "When I talk about your favorite books with you because I know exactly what you enjoy; when we sit by the fire, not even speaking, because the silence feels right; when we laugh until our sides hurt over something silly we saw that raccoon in the wood pile do—"

"That's *not* what I'm talking about!" I cut in, and noticed some people nearby stare at me. I quickly adjusted my voice to a more natural tone. "I mean..." and I trailed off, unsure of how —or perhaps more accurately *if*—I wanted to verbalize anything more.

"Well, I believe those moments are just as important as any other...grander gestures. They're the type of moments that build something more than a mere dance at a party can," Ben said quietly, so quietly, in fact, I almost didn't catch his words. "Also," he said, meeting my eyes directly, his green ones sparkling like emeralds in the chandelier lights above, "you like the codebreaking."

I was fighting within myself at this point, silently

scolding myself for keeping this going. "You give me codes because you can't always talk to me in person, or simply ask me to dance like Gabriel did," I insisted, and even as I said that, I didn't believe my own words.

"That's not why I give you codes at all," Ben said, his words growing just a tad more heated again as he heaved an exaggerated sigh. "I don't send you codes because that's the *only* way I can communicate with you. I send you those codes because that's a way I *can* communicate with you. Don't you get it?"

I stared at him dumbly.

"Look around you," he said, practically spinning me around the room. "You think any of these other people would enjoy expanding their minds like that? Enjoy the adventures we've made for ourselves in our little corner of the world? Enjoy creating those codes—because you've created just as many as I have, let's not forget. Or just enjoy learning?" He grabbed both of my shoulders and spun me so that I was facing him squarely, then stepped close so that I thought for one mad moment he was going to kiss me. "You have...*many* admirable qualities, Eloise," he practically whispered. "But I also value your adventurous spirit and your intellect—quite the underrated qualities if you ask me. And *that's* why I give you codes. I could never send them to most people I meet, and plus, I always thought you liked them?" He ended on a question. It was my turn to speak, but I just stood there, all of my thoughts and feelings colliding within me like a miniature war.

He sighed lightly, turned around, and put my drink down on a nearby decorative table. Turning back to face me, he said, "I can be direct too. Would you like to dance?" he asked, holding out his hand.

My thoughts were still spinning, but I heard my voice say "yes," and I put my hand in his. And as he walked me out to the dance floor and put his other hand on my waist, I felt suddenly like I could melt. All of the anger drained from my body, and I smiled at him. Seeing that, he smiled back, a close-lipped, almost shy smile, but a smile nonetheless. The dance was a calm one, and as we lightly twirled, I leaned in a little closer than necessary. "You're right," I spoke quietly and deliberately. "I do like the coded messages."

Ben's smile grew bigger.

"Come on and dance! You've got the only girl here after all!" Harold said, slapping John on the back in an unusual display of joviality. All of our men had made it out of the woods and were set up in varying degrees of closeness to a bonfire, which the Northerners had made for us. Spirits were high, and despite the exhaustion I knew the men must be feeling, we stayed up late, eating and exchanging stories with our new comrades.

"No, I don't think we will," John answered Harold, though he at least took my hand in his then.

"Oh, come on," Harold said. "They've got an excellent fiddle—" but he cut himself off at whatever look John had shot him. As Harold made his retreat toward another group of men who were laughing raucously, John leaned in and whispered to me, "I don't wish to appear undignified as my first act as leader of what amounts to *two* companies."

"Of course," I responded automatically, my mind elsewhere.

John stood then and moved from group to group, exchanging words and effectively killing the joyful mood of any group he visited. *He has to take himself less seriously*, I silently reflected.

The fiddle music eventually slowed and stopped altogether as men started to fall asleep out in the open and in various corners of the farmstead. The night was warm and the moon was full, illuminating their sleeping bodies.

I was considering following the lead of the soldiers when a man stepped over to me. He looked familiar, with a dark complexion and eyes that reflected the dancing flames of the bonfire. I tried to place him, but my tired brain struggled to do so. "We have the farmhouse over there available to you, miss," he said, his voice gruff and serious despite the otherwise welcoming nature of his words.

"Oh? Thank you," I said, standing so as to follow the man.

"Where are you going?" a nearby voice stopped us. It was John; I hadn't even seen him approach.

"This man said I can stay in the farmhouse," I explained.

"Much comfier for the lady," the soldier said, his head bent.

"Oh, wonderful. I'm tired of sleeping on the ground," John said at once.

The man simply cocked his head in question, but as John did not elaborate the soldier said, "I'm sorry. I was not aware that the two of you are…"

"Married," John answered, and my eyes opened wide. I saw the soldier look at me, and I quickly wiped the expression from my face.

"Well, you're lucky, Captain," the man said, turning back around to lead the way to the farmhouse. "Not many men are fortunate enough to travel with their wives."

"True," John agreed amicably enough, and we started to walk to the house, only a minute away.

"We have a downstairs guestroom here," the soldier said, opening the front door on the dark interior, a single lamp having been lit to guide our path. There were steep stairs off to the left, situated behind what I thought might be a kitchen. Straight ahead of us was a thin, almost oppressive hallway leading to a room at the back of the modest house.

"Thank you," John said with a stern nod of his head, effectively dismissing the soldier. John then picked up the lamp to guide our way down the hallway, toward the pitch-black room at the end.

The hallway seemed to have a rather ridiculous amount of furniture shoved into it, hallway tables, bookcases, and large wardrobes making the entire space feel rather suffocating.

I expected to find the bedroom at the back similarly furnished, but it was much simpler, with a desk and chair, bed, armoire, and a built-in closet in the corner. "Very nice," John said. He walked over to the desk, lit a candle with the lantern, and stepped back into the hallway to place the lantern on one of the tables. "Now, I'm going to retrieve our belongings if you'd like to get yourself out of that dress. You're covered in sap still," he said, and he walked out of the bedroom and down the lit hall.

Instead, I merely paced back and forth, wondering at John's intentions. We were most definitely *not* married. Was this his way of trying to bypass a ceremony? Did he wish to skip the ceremony with no legal bindings? Born of a sudden impulse, I slammed the bedroom door and continued my pacing.

Regardless of how long John was actually gone for, he was back too soon. "I'm back, Eloise," I heard him call. "I have our belongings," he said, and his voice was in high spirits, I noted. I backed against the wall, only realizing then that this small room had no windows.

The bedroom doorknob began to turn, and then there was a knock at what sounded like the front door. "Oh, what now?" John grumbled, immediately preceding a loud thud as he must have thrown down our belongings somewhere in the hall.

Talking ensued down the hallway while I remained pinned to the wall. After a few seconds, "Eloise! It's Harold. He's ready to send word to the army about our success. I just need to write a quick note. I'll be back in just a couple of minutes!"

And then more silence. I still hadn't moved from against the wall, and my heart thudded loudly in my chest; I would have sworn I could see the fabric of my dress moving along with it.

"What to do, what to do, what to do," I repeated over and over to myself, mumbling my words as they came out more in groans than syllables. Spotting the nearby closet, I suddenly dashed toward it and shut myself in.

"This is stupid," I actually said to myself as I hid amongst a few musty coats. "Like sitting in the closet is going to help me." I actually began to laugh at myself a bit, despite my predicament.

Just then, a nearby gunshot rang out.

CHAPTER
TWENTY-ONE

The Battle

I froze, forgetting to breathe and think, the sound of the gunshot not making sense in any way. Inside the closet, everything was silent, muffled. I strained my ears, too afraid to move. I thought I could hear someone—or was it multiple people?—shouting then. Followed by more silence.

My heart resumed its beating, and I took deep, steadying breaths. Perhaps it was just a drunk soldier, or someone firing at a rabbit, I told myself. I had to focus on more pressing matters.

And then the world outside my closet exploded in chaos.

Gunshots, multiple and many, could be heard. They were outside the house, I knew, but I still immediately dropped even lower on the floor, curled into myself like a small rodent. This time, the gunshots didn't stop, and persistent waves shook the house. A larger boom went off, and the entire house quite literally shook with the weight of it. My ears rang as I heard something shatter quite nearby, sounding almost just outside the closet.

The gunshots and shouting continued, and I tried to make sense of it all, my thoughts racing in the dark closet.

It didn't add up. Who would be shooting at us?

Unless the Union army had arrived? I thought of Ben,

wondered what sorts of reinforcements he might have at his disposal.

But even so, John had made sure to station lookouts around the perimeter. Unless they were captured or killed before they could sound the alarm...but could Union soldiers really get right up to the farm that quickly? Would the gunshots sound different if some were coming from farther away and some were coming from close by?

My thoughts swirled, interrupted and jarred by more shooting, more shouts, and one more boom that shook the house. Explosives? Surely not one of the cannons, I told myself.

No, the farm was in the *middle* of fields. An army would have a difficult, if not impossible, time sneaking up on us. And the moon was full, the night bright.

What was happening?

The initial firing had slowed slightly by this point, but only to a steady stream as opposed to an all-out barrage. Screams could still be heard, and my mind perhaps did an even better job of painting the violence for me than a window could have. I could practically see the men getting torn apart with each scream that made its way to my darkened corner. A few gunshots sounded on the house, and I screamed and covered my head with my hands.

No, this couldn't be a surprise attack from soldiers, even as near as the woods. This was something else entirely.

And then suddenly, as if I had been deliberately thinking on the matter, the soldier who had led me and John to the house pulled himself to the forefront of my thoughts. The dark one who looked familiar, only he wasn't dressed like a farmer any longer. I could see him clearly in a Union uniform, his dark eyes dangerous and determined.

I resisted the immediate urge to sit up upon my realization. Instead, wide-eyed on the closet floor, I whispered to myself, barely above the rushing sound in my ears, "The soldier from Miston."

That is what had happened! The Union army hadn't

come from behind and attacked. They had *beaten* us here and disguised themselves as the very men we thought were helping us, the men we thought were new recruits.

Which meant that they had waited, waited until the Confederate soldiers were tired, spread out, and surrounded.

If my assumption was correct, that would also mean that there were approximately equal numbers of men on both sides. But the Union had had the element of surprise, and quite possibly an advantageous physical position, perhaps even keeping some of the finer, newer guns for themselves in anticipation of this moment.

The gunshots were growing quieter, I thought. But then again...perhaps it was only that a new sound was growing louder. A crackling sound, like broken twigs, or crunching hay. Emboldened, I raised my head just slightly, looking around me in the darkness. My eyes had adjusted only enough to see masses above me—hanging coats—but not with any distinct form. The crackling continued, so close I thought it must be in the closet with me. Slowly I reached up and felt for the closet doorknob. Finding it, I turned it and peered out. The lone candle in the middle of the desk was still standing strong, but the room looked hazy. Smoky? It was too much for one candle.

A few gunshots sent me sprawling on the floor again, but I stayed on my side, hearing the crackling sound grow in intensity and watching the light haze at the top of the room.

There was too much to keep up with, too much to process. I felt slow, and tired, as if this were all a dream. Carefully, I crawled into the room like a snake with my stomach on the ground. A massive crash very nearby shook the house again, but this time I was certain the crash had originated *within* the house. Were soldiers inside then? I debated returning to the closet, but the crackling sound had grown with the crash, and it took my befuddled brain only another moment to realize what was happening.

"Fire," I whispered to myself. Pulling myself along on my stomach quickly now, I reached the bedroom door. The crack underneath was brightly lit, and sparks were visible. I put my hand against the wooden door and immediately pulled it back from the intense heat.

Suddenly, the apparent war outside was secondary on my list of immediate dangers. I actually stood then and looked wildly around the room as yet another crash within the house spelled out the danger I was in.

Spinning around, I grabbed the quilt from the bed and whipped it toward the bedroom door. Holding it over the doorknob, I slowly pulled the door open a crack, and flames immediately began licking their way inside the guestroom.

I could immediately see the sources of the crashes—two of the tall spindly bookcases had fallen across the hall, making a sort of slanted obstacle of fire. But there was no going over or under, as the side tables and even a trunk were also now on fire, blocking every possible path to the exit. I barely had a line of sight to the front door, as it disappeared and reappeared only with the dancing of the flames atop the fallen bookcases.

I tried to shut the bedroom door again, but the weight of the closest bookcase had shifted just slightly and was pushing into the doorframe, making shutting it again impossible. Instead, I was forced to leave the door open at an angle as smoke now poured into the room. My lungs began burning, and I dropped once more to the floor, trying to avoid the worst of it.

Just then, above everything, I heard a man's voice, loud and panicked. "Eloise!"

"Ben!" I called back, and I stood up into the smoke, craning my neck to see down the hallway. But, in a brief gap in the flames, it was not Ben's face looking back at me, but John's.

He might not have heard my call, but he saw me then, lines of panic on his face and something dark—blood maybe— dripping down one of his temples.

"I—I don't know—" he stammered, coughing like crazy. "The oil lamp," he said, and I caught a glimpse of him gesturing toward where the end table used to be.

I filled in the blanks. How the shaking of the house must

have knocked over the oil lamp and started the fire. Perhaps John himself had put it too close to the edge, or maybe he had even bumped it slightly as he went to write his message. Regardless, the damage was done.

"Help me move these bookcases," I screamed over the roar of the fire. I wasn't sure John heard me at first, as he merely looked in my direction hopelessly.

I turned, however, and grabbed the chair at the desk. The bookcases would be too hot to touch, but maybe I could start prying them away with the chair.

I started pushing the chair against one of the bookcases, but it was heavier than it looked. It didn't even budge.

"John!" I called, seeing that I was making no progress. But when I saw his face again through the smoke and flames, he was still just standing there, his mouth covered in the crook of his arm, coughing. He had nothing in his hands, wasn't trying to help me in the slightest.

Catching my eyes, burning and dry in the heat, he uncovered his mouth only briefly. "I'm sorry! I have to try to make it to safety at this point!"

Armed with one of the new guns from the barn, he turned his back on me then.

"No!" I screamed loud and long, but he didn't look back. The flames rose even higher. My throat burned with the effort of having screamed, and I began choking. But just then, the flames parted, allowing me to see John one last time. He had made it to the door of the farmhouse, his weapon extended toward the outside. I heard a shot ring out, and saw John collapse immediately on the front step.

CHAPTER TWENTY-TWO

Captured

I collapsed only a second later.

Everything sounded far off, like it were coming to me from under a blanket. I strained for air, and finally, on the floor, I started to feel just a bit enter my lungs. I took small breaths, necessarily, though I desperately wanted more.

The flames were beginning to enter the bedroom as well as the smoke. I was in a wooden house, after all.

I detachedly wondered how the battle had gone outside. Had my role in all of this made a difference? Did I help do anything? I figured, at that moment, quite calmly, that I would never truly know.

When I had started on my journey to Virginia, I had figured there was a very real chance that something might happen to me. I might be shot, discovered, hung, or molested. But, oddly enough, I never once considered the possibility of dying in a fire. Funny how life throws things like that at us sometimes, things we wouldn't have thought likely or possible, I mused.

I swallowed once, using spit I didn't know I had, and suddenly, I heard a call. "Eloise!"

Had John come back? That was my first thought, but I immediately remembered his fallen body in the doorframe. I took a breath of air, managing to keep it in and my lungs calm.

"Eloise!" There it was again.

"Ben?" I questioned, just loud enough for my own ears.

"Eloise! Are you in here?" came the frantic scream again.

And for the first time in all of this—for the first time since I said goodbye to him on that cold, fall day, standing at the lake, a weight in my heart—I heard Ben's voice.

"Ben!" I called louder, taking another steadying breath of air and pushing myself up. I coughed with the effort. I reached for the quilt, but saw that part of it was already on fire. Going back for the pillow, I held it up to my face, staying hunched over as I made my way back to the blocked door. "Ben!" I screamed, removing the pillow for a moment.

He was standing where John had been only a minute before. Our eyes locked, and for a brief second, we both smiled despite the destruction and death around us.

"I'm going to get you out!" he said then, and he started scanning around him wildly. He was gone then, covered by the flames and smoke, but when I caught a glimpse of him again, he had what appeared to be a broken rocking chair in his hands, and he was using it to push flaming objects out of the way. I saw him only intermittently for the next minute, though I heard his coughing. Panic seized me. Would we *both* die in here?

He was still halfway down the hallway, hitting and moving objects. And I was inside, blocked by a heavy bookcase I knew I couldn't work on on my own. I was, not for the first time, feeling helpless in all of this.

Dropping low for a moment to take a desperately needed breath of air, I hit my head slightly on the desk. It was a small bump, the least of my worries, and I didn't bother moving my head more than a couple of inches back from it as I gulped more air.

I had knocked one of the drawers open just slightly, though, and for who knows what reason, I looked inside of it.

Paper.

More tinder for the fire, was my cynical first thought. But then a second one occurred to me as I took in my situation—a fire in the house and a war outside. Frantically, I withdrew a piece of paper and a writing instrument, and I began scribbling.

"Eloise! Are you still there?" Ben's voice, frantic, asked a minute later.

"Yes!" I screamed back, and I poked my head up for a moment to see that he had made progress. He was moving the farthest bookcase before the one blocking my own door, and struggling to do so. Still, as there was nothing I could do about that particular situation, I dropped to the floor again and kept writing, hoping against the dire predicament we found ourselves in.

I heard a loud crash then. Hastily, I folded the paper sloppily and actually shoved it down the front of my dress. When I stood, I saw that Ben had managed not so much to move the fiery bookcase as to break it in half, now a flaming obstacle to jump over rather than be blocked by entirely. But that still left the slanted one before me, blocked on the underside by a flaming table. Even as I thought that, though, I realized that the table was no longer there. It had crumbled in on itself, leaving large splinters of fiery wood in its stead.

"Ben, toss me the chair!" I said, nodding toward what was left of the broken rocking chair he had been using. Not questioning me, he immediately did so, it barely making it through the flames above the bookshelf. I had stepped back, allowing it to pass, and as I picked it off the floor, I noticed how charred it was, but still broken in a more suitable way than the whole chair I had been using previously. Taking the good end, the end Ben must have been holding, I began pressing on the back of the bookshelf, hoping to break it in two, much like Ben had. It was fully on fire, but still solid. I had one more idea, though. I quickly shoved it under the bookshelf, knocking the burning remains of the side table to the ground. Then, as quickly as I could, I threw down what was left of the rocking chair and began to undress. I was down to my drawers, chemise, and traveling corset in a minute, my fingers flying over buttons and laces.

Then, I stole over to the bed, grabbing the last blanket in the vicinity that wasn't on fire, and, wrapping it around my body and over my head, I dove into the small, fiery space between the wall and under the slanted bookshelf. I moved quickly. I would catch on fire in a moment, I knew, even with the bulkiest of my clothes removed. Popping my head up on the other side of the bookshelf, I saw Ben's surprised face; clearly he hadn't been expecting to see me quite literally in the middle of the fire. I reached out my arm to roll over the burning bookshelf flattened in front of Ben when I touched something with my arm and let out a scream of pain.

"Wait!" Ben screamed, and I saw that he was holding a quilt of his own, possibly retrieved from upstairs. Tossing it then across the burning, horizontal bookshelf, I knew I would only have a second before it too was eaten up by the flames. Ducking my head within my quilt, I rolled across it and onto the floor beside Ben. I threw off the quilt, which was most definitely on fire in at least one area, and Ben grabbed my hand as we dashed toward the front door.

But John's body lay as a stumbling block at the threshold, and before I could even consider my actions, I was down on the floor next to him, feeling for a pulse.

"I'm sorry!" Ben practically screamed at me, wincing, the fire loud and still close. "I had to shoot him or be shot."

My supporting hand had slipped in a pool of blood around his side as I felt for his pulse with the other. Nothing.

I looked at his face. His eyes were still open as if defying death, the one side illuminated by fire, the other by the bright light of the full moon.

"Let's go," I said, standing and carefully stepping over his body, reaching out for and taking Ben's hand, now also sticky with blood.

Outside, I still heard sporadic gunfire and shouts.

"Quick!" Ben called into my ear. "We have to get you someplace safe until the fighting is over." And he took off to the right as fast as he could go, pulling me with him.

There was a fairly wide open space to this side before a field of cornstalks rose up. We ran at full speed for a minute before we reached the cornstalks. By the time we had only made it a few rows deep, I collapsed to the ground, coughing and gasping for air.

"Eloise!" Ben said, dropping down next to me, but as he did so, he too started coughing. The fit passed in a minute, though, and we both rested there breathing the much fresher air in the cornfield, on our hands and knees, staring into the earth.

As we crouched there, I heard more shouts than gunfire. Whatever had happened was coming to a close.

I took more relaxed gasps of air, pushing myself into a seated position. Ben followed suit, stripping off his coat and throwing it to the ground nearby before scrutinizing my face as I did the same to him.

My goodness, I could only imagine what I looked like if Ben looked this bad. His hair was a bit shorter than usual, though it still had its strong, noticeable waves. But his face was covered in smoke and soot, as was his white shirt. He had a deep gash on his cheek from which blood had trickled downward onto the collar of his shirt. His hands were bleeding in multiple areas, and his pants were torn and charred around the ankles.

And for all of that, I knew I must have looked even stranger, sitting there in smoke-colored, burnt drawers and other bare essentials, with a tingling burn mark on my arm and half my hair coming out of what was once a respectable bun.

I was on the verge of laughing, the night's events far too overwhelming to deal with yet on any deeper level, but apparently Ben was not of the same mind.

"I'm sorry I killed him," Ben said again, and it took me a moment to understand where his mind still was. "I...he clearly must have meant something to you after spending all of that time with him, and he kept saying you were married?" Ben grimaced and looked as if he were about to be physically ill as he held his stomach.

I shook my head slowly. "No, we weren't married. Just a convenient lie he made up for his own gratification. He…he always thought he could take what he wanted. You should have seen him throw his supposed best friend to the wolves in the hope of obtaining a promotion. And I…well, I believe I was just a means to an end for him. My skills made him look good, and he wished to cultivate that. But…I suppose I took advantage of him in the same way. We're even."

Ben's face had hardened as I had explained. "Except that you tried to save him at the end. He wasn't really about to leave you for dead, was he?" Ben pressed.

I swallowed, remembering that feeling of total abandonment as I had watched John turn his back on me and head for the front door. I nodded my head and smirked then, for I had made it out after all. As I did so, I realized that the sound of the burning farmhouse was now the only one reaching us out in the field.

I looked up at Ben, who had indeed not only met me in Turnersville, but had helped save me. I reached out my hand for his, and he took it hesitantly. "What's wrong?" I asked, looking down at his scratched hand.

"Did he hurt you? I…I've been so afraid ever since you left for Virginia that you would be hurt."

I straightened my back and looked him directly in the eyes, the moonlight illuminating the stalks around us and making Ben, even seated as we were, easy enough to see. "I went of my own free will, Benjamin West," I spoke in sharp staccatos. With a sigh, I continued more tenderly. "I knew the dangers of spying on the Confederate army. But I needed to help, especially after Ethan's death. You *knew* that, and you gave me a purpose." I thought back to all of our letters, and how we had needed to be one step ahead, or one step deeper, than anyone would have considered for our ruse to work. How we at times needed to infer meanings between us, or hide a message *within* a hidden message. "And to answer your question, no, I was not hurt by Captain John Cardis." The tension in Ben's shoulders immediately left him. I paused for just a second. "He *did* kiss me," I said slowly. "But that's it."

The tension played with Ben again for a moment before he sighed. "I tried to keep you safe from *him* as well as from the army."

I smiled. "I know, and you *did*. Thank you for sending those soldiers into the inn back in Miston and scaring us off from there. It saved me from some...alone time with John."

He nodded his head. "I'm glad that worked."

"And tonight the battle couldn't have begun at a better time."

He smiled just a little and scratched at the back of his neck. He looked like he did when he was a boy, having just beaten me at a card game, a little impressed with himself. "Yeah...I may have been responsible for moving up the battle by an hour or two when I saw you head to the farmhouse with him."

I smiled at him, and then looked down at my knees, suddenly aware again that I was in my most comfortable—and worn—corset, chemise, and drawers. In short, I looked entirely inappropriate, not to mention bloody and dirty. "I...I look ridiculous," I said, my voice tinged with both horror and laughter.

Ben looked at me, and I thought he blushed a bit under all of the smoke and blood streaked across his face. "Well, it's better than burning to a crisp fully clothed," he said with a shrug and a hint of his usual, mischievous smile. Though, more like a gentleman, he added, "I'll make sure we find you something suitable to wear once we go back."

There hadn't been a single gunshot in over a minute, though we could still hear the fire. I wondered if there would be anything left of the house by the time it stopped.

"How was the battle going?" I asked, realizing that we might not be out of danger yet.

"Oh, unless something wildly unexpected has occurred,

we were doing just fine. We armed ourselves with a liberal amount of the new weaponry ahead of time—repeating arms and whatnot—and we made sure we were in good positions with plenty of cover before the fighting began. We also, very sneakily I might add, didn't drink anything so we would be prepared, and we were all as well-rested as possible, whereas the Confederates were not?" This last bit was a question, and I nodded my head to confirm his assumptions. "Anyway, when Captain Cardis came out to send the message, we sprung our trap, drawing our weapons and demanding he surrender. He...well...he didn't, which I can't say was very smart on his part. A lot of men died unnecessarily." Ben licked his cracked lips, and I suddenly couldn't wait to hopefully find some water. "Anyway, he was able to duck behind a barrel when the shooting started, which is why he was able to return to you, at least for a moment."

"And then he was in the process of running away when you shot him," I cut in.

"He seemed that sort to me, though I assume he would have had one wild story of his bravery to relay to his superiors." He heaved a sigh and coughed again for a bit. "Anyway," he said, catching his breath, "several men were killed from the gunfire and explosives, but we were starting to take quite a few prisoners instead, and by the time I realized the house was on fire and you needed my help, it seemed at least as if there was no way we could lose. So, I truly anticipate finding the situation well in hand upon our return."

"And the supplies?"

He shrugged. "Assuming they're not burnt up if the fire spreads," he said, uneasy for a moment, "they'll be nice to have, though probably not essential for the Union army. We are well supplied. The Confederates are too, really, but if they're going to be making a push into hostile territory, some of the more advanced weaponry may have meant quite the advantage for them. And reliable and plentiful ammunition for some of those more advanced weapons is something they surely could have made use of."

"So we made a difference here?" I asked.

"I do believe so," he said, his smile calm and familiar. "You did a great job."

I smiled back, and felt a wave of calm rush over me.

"There hasn't been any more gunfire for a bit," Ben said after a moment. "Perhaps we should at least make our way back to the very edge of the cornfield so we can try to see what's happening."

"All right," I said, and he stood and helped me up with minimal coughing by either of us.

He moved his body as if to turn in the direction of the farm, but I stopped him. "Wait, Ben," I said, and he looked at me. I stood on tiptoe and raised my head toward his. In an instant, he followed my actions, and leaned down and kissed me.

It was nothing like the first kisses of which I had heard, taking place on romantic strolls in the family garden or under the shade of a beautiful old tree, it's branches waving in the wind. It was smoke-scented and sudden, and the tang of blood filled my nostrils. But I wished it could go on forever. It was me and Ben, and despite everything else, it was the most perfect thing in the world.

As our lips finally pulled apart, Ben looked down into my eyes and practically whispered, deep and sincere, "I love you."

I parted my lips to say it back when I heard a metallic click, and a man's voice broke through the night. "I wouldn't say one other word if I were you."

We looked to our side where, just barely coming into view from behind the cornstalks, one of the soldiers, Harold, stood with his gun aimed directly at my heart. Ben immediately stood ready to fight, but with nothing at all in his own hands, he looked decidedly less menacing.

"I heard the end of whatever little conversation you two had been having," Harold said, his voice hoarse and his brown hair sticking up in all directions. As he held the gun out, another man came up beside him, similarly armed with a pointed gun.

"You whore," Harold said, all of his anger focused on me,

his voice shaking. "John *loved* you, and now he's dead."

I knew there was very little, if any, truth in his statement, but deemed it wiser to stay quiet just yet.

"You know, I *knew* you were a traitor the whole time," he continued.

"No you didn't," I said at once. Now, that was true, I thought cockily, but I had better continue quickly, I determined. "You couldn't have known that because it simply isn't true."

"Oh, yeah?" he said, taking another step forward, the gun remaining focused on my heart. "So you just happened to fall into this pretender here, who happened to decided *now* was the right time to profess his love for you?"

"Do you know who this is?" I said, with a sideways nod of my head. "This is Ben West."

It took Harold a moment of recognition before he swiveled his gun to Ben's heart instead, and for a brief panicked moment I thought he would discharge it then. "Wait! You'll want him alive. He knows too much."

"Maybe. But *you* don't know too much," he said, swinging his gun—oddly thankfully—back in my direction."

"I know his codes, like I always have."

"Which mean nothing to us now, as the two of you are working together," Harold said, spitting in the dirt in front of me.

"Are we?" I asked, and Harold raised his eyebrows and cocked his head.

"What do you mean?"

"You saw us kissing, I presume?" I asked, my voice growing steadier and calmer despite the gun. I could practically feel Ben's eyes darting all around us, but Harold and the other soldier's guns were only a few feet away—there was no chance of outrunning them, and next to no chance of successfully tackling them before at least one could discharge his weapon.

"Yes, I saw you kissing," Harold said, and as his muscles clenched, I worried for a moment that he would squeeze the trigger, even accidentally.

I winced, but forced myself to continue. "And there was a purpose to that," I said, and I hoped that I was portraying confidence. "I swiped this from his pants pocket as we kissed," I said, pulling out a crumpled note from between my breasts where I had stuffed it back in the burning farmhouse.

"I didn't see you swipe anything," Harold said, his eyes narrowed at me.

"That's good because then I wouldn't have been able to take it from Ben without *him* noticing either," I said offhandedly. "So...do you want me to break it for you? Tell you what you need to know?"

Harold and the other man exchanged the briefest of glances, though not long enough for me or Ben to actually act on the pause. "No, we'll take it. Throw it here," Harold said, and I tossed it on the ground in front of him, the other soldier pointing his gun at Ben hard while Harold stooped to pick it up. Unfolding it in the slanted light of the receding full moon, Harold kept his gun pointed at us as best he could.

"What is this nonsense?" he muttered to himself.

"I can break the code for you," I offered, "being as we're still on the same side."

"We'll determine that *later*," Harold said.

"Oh, this is a simple one, I think," the other soldier spoke up, gazing at the paper over Harold's shoulder. See that? This probably is a letter of the alphabet, and that represents the movement," he said, pointing at the paper, and I smiled.

"It might be harder than you think," I offered.

"Nonsense. You must think we're stupid," Harold said.

"Well, it's just that I'm a woman who has had a lot of training in breaking codes, unlike you soldiers," I put in. If they weren't ready to stand there and solve it now, they never would be.

"Shut up," Harold said, eyeing me again before looking back at the paper.

I chanced a very quick glance at Ben, whose wide eyes met mine, and I threw him the smallest of smirks, causing his shoulders to relax, though I caught his head moving slightly, probably like I was, still trying to think of an actual way out of this predicament.

"So, this first letter would be a T," the other soldier said helpfully.

"Shut up," Harold said. "You think I don't know that?"

I smiled to myself. I may have written the letter hastily, but it would keep them confidently busy for at least a few minutes.

$R \rightarrow 2$

18.6.3 14.19.16.14.13.17.3 13.4 18.6.7.17 11.3.17.17.25.5.3 7.17 18.13

17.7.11.14.10.23 26.19.23 11.3 18.7.11.3

Still, a rescue needed to present itself in those few minutes, or the paper was pointless.

CHAPTER TWENTY-THREE

Modesty

Ethan had always been a sneaky little boy. But it was always in good fun, and strangely enough, we loved him all the more for it. Perhaps, it was because he managed to do the right thing in the end. Like when our father stepped outside, calling for him to come in so he could have his help with fixing the door. Ethan had been with me and Ben just a moment before. But as soon as Father stepped outside, it was as if he had melted away into the air! The second our father had returned to the house, I heard Ethan's triumphant giggling up in a nearby tree. How he had managed to climb out of view so quickly was beyond me.

Nevertheless, that night the door had been fixed, much to my father's surprise. Ethan had always been exceptionally handy, even in our youth.

Ethan was ten years old when what Ben and I deemed "The Great Cookie Heist" occurred. My goodness, we still joked about it, even as young adults.

"Mm, mm. Mrs. Brown, what are you cooking in here?" Ben had asked, sauntering into the kitchen where my mother was hard at work baking while I mended some clothing nearby.

"Gingersnaps, but they're not for us," I answered for my mother automatically.

"Aw, why?" Ben asked, stepping forward and reaching for one of the cooling cookies before my mother playfully slapped his hand away.

"They're for the Thompsons," my mother said. "They're having a little party for Heather who just had a baby. I'm bringing these for the women to share."

"Aw, but can't we just have one each? No one will even notice they're gone," Ben said, his face down at the level of the cookies.

"Benjamin West, you stop breathing all over my cookies," my mother said sternly, though her eyes still sparkled with merriment.

Ben stood and shrugged his shoulders, coming over to sit next to me at the table. "You got closer than Ethan at least. He barely stepped into the room and my mother sent him out again."

"And it was totally uncalled for!" Ethan yelled from the parlor.

"Okay. Last batch," my mother announced, sliding cookies off of a pan to cool. Only a couple minutes later, Ethan entered, wearing one of my father's coats, the sleeves completely covering his hands, and the shoulders appearing more shawl-like than fitted on his small frame.

"Ethan Brown, what on earth are you doing in your father's coat?" my mother asked, still holding a pan with a few remaining cookies.

"I don't feel so good. I feel a little chilled, so I put on father's coat since it was the nearest thing," he said, sniffling once.

My mother set the pan down and immediately went over to him. She leaned forward and touched his forehead to her cheek. "You feel fine," she said, eyeing him skeptically.

"I don't know," he said, stepping toward the counter with the cookies and pulling up a seat, staring at them wistfully.

"I hope this isn't a ploy to steal any of the gingersnaps," my mother said, crossing her arms.

"Of course not," Ethan said, but he was now looking past my mother toward me. "Eloise, I saw you drop something small. Was it a spare needle?"

All eyes in the room were suddenly on me. "I don't think so," I said, searching around me.

"It looked like it landed near your heel," Ethan insisted.

Ben immediately dropped to the floor near me, and my mother helped as I checked my lap thoroughly. "I'm fairly certain I only had the two needles, and they're both right here," I insisted.

After perhaps only ten seconds of fruitless searching, my mother stood up. "Wait a minute. Ethan Brown, stand up," she said, spinning around and pursing her lips. "Show me your hands immediately."

Ethan stood up and held out his arms, both hands completely concealed in the sleeves.

"No," she said slowly, smirking. "Show me your hands *under* the sleeves."

At this point, Ben and I were both snickering.

But Ethan was unbothered. He held his arms out in front of him, and shook the sleeves down his arms, revealing his perfectly empty hands. Then, for good show, he held onto one sleeve and shook it out toward the floor while both hands remained visible, and then he repeated the action on the other side.

My mother looked at him sideways. "Okay, leave the kitchen before I suspect you of any other thefts," she said, and Ethan obeyed, heading toward the parlor. But just before he crossed the kitchen threshold, his eye caught mine and made the quickest of winks.

"I'm going to make sure he's comfortable since he's not feeling well," I said quickly, and Ben immediately followed.

In the parlor, Ethan sat down in front of the sofa, concealed from the door to the hallway. Ben and I silently followed him where he hurriedly produced three gingersnaps from father's coat pocket. He handed us each one and whispered mischievously, his eyes squinted and laughing, "I wanted the coat for the large pockets, not the *sleeves*."

"Isn't Father going to find it odd when he has crumbs in his coat pocket?" I whispered, eating the still-warm treat as we giggled conspiratorially.

"I'll shake it out first," Ethan said with a shrug of his shoulders. We munched away happily on our hard-won treats. I could have sworn I heard a stifled laugh from the direction of the hallway, but I was never sure, and I never asked.

Harold and the other soldier seemed to be making surprisingly slow progress, though I could still hear them offering each other letters to make words. "So that would make this letter an S," Harold was saying matter-of-factly.

I shot a quick glance at Ben. I noticed his eyes darting around madly, but I had to give Harold's power of concentration credit—he hadn't relaxed his outstretched gun the entire time, as it remained steadily focused on my heart.

Ben, noticing my eyes, looked at me. "I'm sorry," he said sadly.

"Shut up!" Harold said at once, jerking his arm slightly to emphasize the weapon he still held.

Ben looked heartbroken, his dirty face no longer triumphant, but worn. His shoulders slumped and his breathing came in sighs of defeat.

But how had this happened? I asked myself that. How had we gone from fighting for our lives just a short distance away to powerless in a cornfield? I mentally stepped through our actions, my eyes locked on Ben's the whole time, almost willing for them to explain the situation to me.

A breeze swept through the field and I felt a momentary chill, reminding me of my current state of undress. And suddenly, I understood.

"So then this letter is an M," the other soldier was saying.

I winked at Ben and noticed his eyes widen in surprise.

"Harold," I said strongly, turning to face him and the barrel of his gun.

Harold didn't speak, but merely glared at me. I continued. "You may not have noticed, but I'm not wearing any clothes really," I said, motioning toward my limited undergarments.

Even in the darkness broken only by the flames in the near distance, I could see Harold's eyes dart across me uncomfortably. "I'm trying not to look as I was raised a gentleman," he said.

"Indeed," I said slowly, aware that all eyes were on me. "I unfortunately came to be in this current state after a series of events regarding the house fire," I said. "So, given that you are, as you put it, a gentleman, I was hoping you'd allow me to reach for the coat there on the ground," I said, nodding toward Ben's coat next to Harold. "I really do wish to be a bit more modest than this. And especially after you decipher that message and find that I *am* on your side, you're going to want things between us to be as professional as possible."

"Fine," he said, and he jerked his head in the direction of Ben's coat, keeping his gun focused on me the entire time. I heard Ben make a noise, almost like a quiet whimper as the gun followed my hesitant steps forward.

Picking up the coat, I quickly hurried back to my position next to Ben before I put it on, once again all eyes on me. "Thank you," I said, wrapping it around myself tightly, my arms tucked in it around my body.

Apparently satisfied, Harold's eyes returned to the letter. "What's he purchasing?" the other soldier asked.

"Shut up so I can focus and find out," Harold said.

The other soldier paid him no mind. "See?" he instead asked, his face practically joyful. "We don't need her anyway. We're doing just fine on our own."

My hand slid slowly inside the coat further, hitting upon the hard object I assumed had been stowed there following our escape. I could only hope it was one of the new repeating ones that wouldn't require an immediate reload.

Ben had practically stopped breathing next to me. His eyes were wide and his body tense. I was close to him, but not close enough to receive assistance unnoticed.

Slowly, so as not to attract attention, I fastened my hand on the gun that was concealed in Ben's interior coat pocket. Barely pulling it out, and careful to keep it concealed by the coat, I readied it in my right hand, all while keeping my arms wrapped in front of me, as if I were merely chilly.

"I think there's only one more word," Harold announced. But he never got to decipher that last word as I whipped out the gun and fired at him first. I barely had time to register the surprised eyes of the other soldier before firing at him as well.

Ben and I both ran over to them, Ben kicking the guns away from their hands. It was unnecessary, though. The shots had done their work immediately, through their chests.

Ben turned to me at once. He hugged me to him close, though he was shaking violently the whole time. "It's all right," I whispered, and I couldn't quite tell who was trying to console whom.

"Where'd you learn to shoot like that?" he asked, even his voice shaking.

"I didn't," I said, and a small, panicky laugh could be felt in Ben's chest against my head.

"I couldn't figure out how to lunge for my gun without getting you shot," he said, his voice cracking.

"The Great Cookie Heist," I simply responded, and after a moment, Ben laughed briefly, though this time with less hesitance.

"Oversized coats are great at concealing things," he said. "Though..." he added, releasing me and listening. "I don't care to press our luck again. Let's head back. A long way, I might suggest," he said, scanning the cornstalks around us. "I really do believe we've won, but I'd rather not hang about to let us be taken unawares again."

And grabbing my hand, he pulled me through the

cornstalks as the fire burned up into the sky, overtaking the orange of the rising sun.

CHAPTER TWENTY-FOUR

After Gettysburg

In the beginning of July, Confederate and Union soldiers met at the Battle of Gettysburg. Ben and I weren't there, as we stayed nearby Turnersville, helping coordinate supply transfers to the Union army. But we were assured by contacts of Ben's that what we did made a difference in that horrific battle. His one friend went so far as to say we were the cause of the Confederate retreat back to the South through our depriving them of the modern supplies they were expecting in the North. Neither Ben nor I will go so far as to take credit for that, and clearly the casualties—in the tens of thousands, I believe—did not speak to an undeniable throttling of the Confederate army. However, echoing the sentiments of a different contact's heartfelt letter of thanks, we like to believe that what we did made a difference, however small. Perhaps it simply meant that a group of soldiers were able to return home to their families who might have otherwise been slaughtered by the undeniably capable weaponry we recovered. Either way, we tried our best—for the Union, and in honor of Ethan's memory.

After we finished our business at what remained of the Turnersville Farmstead, Ben and I spent about a month in Harrisburg where we deciphered a total of one intercepted Confederate message. It was at that point that Ben finally earned himself an honorable discharge, and I a much needed rest.

And so at the end of September, Ben and I found ourselves hand-in-hand, walking the last ten miles toward home after taking a train for the bulk of the journey.

As Ben and I walked, he kept remarking about the weather. The wind seemed nearly a visible gray as it whipped my hair, the threat of rain imminent.

"Don't worry about it," I kept reassuring him. "After all we've been through, I doubt we can't handle a little rain."

He finally smiled at me, shrugged light-heartedly, and readjusted the frayed and worn sack that held what was left of his personal belongings.

"Your parents are going to be overjoyed to see you," Ben said as we climbed a very familiar hill near our families' properties.

I laughed uneasily as I remembered the passionate letter I had received in Harrisburg in response to my own letter assuring my mother of my safety, the first I had been able to send since my departure.

"Well, words like 'how dare you leave' didn't paint the happiest picture of a homecoming," I said with a nervous smile.

He lowered his head and looked at me with a smirk. "If the noticeable tear stains on her letter and the five 'I love yous' didn't assure you of a happy homecoming, I'm not sure what will."

I took a deep breath. "No, you're right."

We came to the top of the hill, and spread out below us was our lake and our families' homes situated beyond that.

"We're home," Ben said. And as he spoke, the sky opened up.

"Ah!" I shouted, though my exclamation was not entirely unhappy at that point.

"Come on!" Ben called through the sudden downpour, large droplets quickly soaking through my clothes.

Holding hands, we half-ran, half-slid down the hill, quickly reaching a willow tree near the edge of the lake. We were both laughing, our chests heaving by the time we reached it.

"We can keep going," I said, a huge smile on my face. "I

don't think it's possible to get any more drenched, after all."

The branches and leaves of the willow tree were yellowed, but not yet fallen. It kept out a surprising amount of the rain, though big droplets could still be felt individually, falling on our hair and faces.

"Well, I just wanted you to have something first," Ben said, his smile stretched wide. "Before we go in to see our parents." His green eyes stood out across the flowing canopy of yellow shrouding us in privacy. His tousled, wavy hair moved in the wind, and I felt the peace and happiness of home wash over me.

He reached into his jacket and pulled out a mostly dry piece of paper. He held onto it for a moment, running his fingers over the creased paper thoughtfully before handing it over to me.

I opened it. "Another code?" I asked.

"Go on," he said, and I noticed his hands were shaking just a bit.

I looked down at it, shielding it as best I could against the raindrops, though a few managed to find the paper nevertheless.

"I don't think we've ever done this type before," I said.

"I still know you can do it."

Determined, I looked back at the paper.

Eloise,

Simply continue without lifting from the paper unless directed to do so by the dotted lines.

4 Words

I looked up at him, my gaze direct and my breath coming fast. He reached for his pocket, keeping his eyes on me, both of us shaking and smiling at this point.

And I knew what I had known for a while now, ever since Ben had found me in that burning farmhouse and stood with me in that cornfield: I was truly home.

Solutions

1)   **The Birthday Message:** A young Ben wishes to surprise Eloise with a fun challenge on her birthday due to their mutual love of puzzles and codes. In this simple starter code, Ben makes a number of capitalization "errors." All of the capitalized letters that should not usually be capitalized can be pulled out to create the following message: "I THE INFAMOUS CAPTAIN CUTLER HAVE KIDNAPPED ETHAN YOUR CHALLENGE IS TO SEE THROUGH THE OBVIOUS RIGHT SOLUTION.

The words "see through the obvious right" is a clue in and of itself, as Eloise ultimately must take the not-so-obvious path, going *left* at the lake.

2)   **The Picture of a Man (Ben) with a Scale**: The message is simply a play on words: Wait for me. There are weights on the scale, or "waits." Then you'll notice that one of the weights is labelled specifically "for" Ben, and he is the one who is looking at them in the picture. Therefore, "weight for" can become "wait for." Additionally, there are four weights, so the middle word "for" could be gleaned from this as well. As Ben is the artist and subject of the picture, the "me" can be determined, as it would be from his point of view.

Eloise also gives you a small glimpse into the types of messages Ben has hidden in pictures in the past. For example, the sheep one she mentions would have said "You meet me under the willow tree." You know by this time that there is a willow tree at the lake as it has been briefly mentioned. Additionally, female sheep are known as "ewes," and in this case they are also becoming "meat." As Ben is the one doing the butchering in this picture, he once again uses his self-insertion to mean "me."

3.   **Ben's Letter Following the Loss of Ethan**: Each number corresponds to a letter in the alphabet in order. For example,

1=A, 2=B, 3=C, and so on and so forth. *However*, Ben changed this up slightly by halving each number. Therefore, the word "doubly" in his explanation paragraph is meant to explain that you must double each number in order to get the real number. Therefore, .5 becomes 1, which is A. 1 becomes 2, which is B. 1.5 becomes 3, which is C. Breaking this code should enable you to read the following message: READY YOURSELF FOR I SHALL SOON SEND A WAY THAT YOU CAN HELP WIN THE WAR AND THUS HONOR ETHANS MEMORY BUT IF YOU DO YOU MUST BE VERY CAREFUL

4.   **Ben's Heartbreaking Letter About His Love**: Ben knows, as he even mentions briefly in the letter, that Eloise speaks French. Therefore, he hides his true purpose in an English letter by sprinkling it throughout with French words. Aside from the act of translating this message, the trickiest part of this may be that some French words are spelled the same in English, or have separate English meanings. ("Codes" may have been especially difficult to pull out.) Additionally, words like "a" may appear multiple times. However, even if you pull out all of the a's, you should be able to eliminate the ones that are blatantly unnecessary when forming your French sentence. Finally, accent marks and hyphens have been omitted to help it blend in to the English. While this makes it slightly incorrect, it is understandable in the French language, much as reading "its an example" still makes sense in English without the apostrophe. Therefore, it should ultimately read: va a la ville verte en Virginie ou tu trouveras une compagnie que tu dois connaitre montre leur la lettre et promets leur de dechiffrer mes codes. In English, this should translate to: go to the green town in Virginia where you'll find a company you should get to know show them the letter and promise to decipher my codes.

Ben included a second letter, presumably without a code, so that Eloise could bring it with her to show the soldiers in Virginia without fear of anyone picking up on the French words.

5.   **Ben's Intercepted Letter in Chapter Seven**: If you are stumped, I would strongly recommend reading till the end of the chapter, as some additional and helpful clues are given. That being said, if the suspicious order of the initial greeting was enough to help you get started, you may have realized that this code is a keyword cipher. While having a keyword is common with other, more difficult ciphers, like Playfair Cipher, this one is much more closely related to a traditional Caesar Cipher. The keyword is "Captain Cutler." Skipping repeat letters, you would assign "CAPTINULER" to "ABCDEFGHIJ" in that order. Then you would continue on using the rest of the unused letters. In this case, Ben continued with "BDFGH" and so on, giving those letters "KLMNO." The deciphered letter reads: "CAPTAIN CUTLER, I HAVE INFORMATION REGARDING WEAPONS AND SUPPLIES MEET ME AT CROWS INN WELTON AT THREE ON JANUARY TWENTY SEVEN."

One other final thing to ponder would be the name it was addressed to, Captain Cutler. (If you have not yet realized the name's implication, you may choose to stop reading. Otherwise, the connection will be named plainly here.) Captain Cutler is the name of the childhood character Ben invented and would play at with Eloise.

6.   **Virginie's Letter to Ben**: If you have solved the messages up until this point, you will probably have guessed that Virginie is not a real person, as the name was simply used to direct Eloise to Virginia. As she isn't a real person, you can also assume that the letter is from Ben. Although technically penned by an accomplice according to Ben's directions as it needed to be in a different handwriting, Ben hid a very simple message to Eloise. Skip every other word, and you find the following message: "I love you very much Eloise be encouraged." Eloise burnt the letter afterwards to destroy the message so that it could not be properly read if Captain Cardis were to have more time to do so.

7.   **Apology Letter from Ben**: Ben encloses the key to deciphering this code in the beginning of the letter. He specifically mentions "45 degrees" and that the rain is coming down at a harsh "angle." He also purposefully misspells vortex as vertex. Starting at the word vertex, if you create a 45 degree angle on the page, a message will be clear. Starting from the top right corner, heading to the vertex, and then completing the angle with the horizontal line at the bottom, Ben's real message reads: where are the weapons and soldiers in Pennsylvania that is why your company is waiting <Vertex> Do you love me as I love you? Stay safe in these uncertain times, El.

8.   **Ben's Relative List and Test Phrase**: Ben's phony relative list is a way to exchange secret messages with Eloise specifically, as they are the only ones who know what each phrase combination means. The list works in a sort of "if this, then that" way. So if one of those relatives is mentioned you know the message will be linked to the capitalized words. So:

1. *Uncle Sam in Kentucky=Meet*
   Uncle Sam in Wisconsin=Don't Meet
2. *Aunt Bessie in New York=Yes*
   Aunt Bessie in New Jersey=No
3. *Louis in Pennsylvania=Know*
   Louis in Georgia=Don't Know
4.* *Great Uncle Oscar in Vermont=You are/should*
   Great Uncle Oscar in Rhode Island=You aren't/shouldn't
5.* *Aunt Edna in Massachusetts=I am/should*
   Aunt Edna in Virginia=I am not/shouldn't
6. *Uncle Andrew in Connecticut=Bring*
   Uncle Andrew in Tennessee=Don't bring

   *Note: The words are only "you" and "I." However, the are/ should, etc. are implied. If someone said "you funny," generally you could interpret that to mean "you are funny," even if it sounds a bit

like a caveman. Additionally, "you leave" works the same way with a "should" or "must" being implied between the two words.

Now, Ben also said to pay attention to the numbers. As the phrases only point to specific verbs and nouns, Ben used the numbers from the list as a way to complete the thought. After the state is mentioned in conjunction with these people, you can count that many words past the state to arrive at the combination. So, Ben's test message to Eloise actually reads: "You (are) smart. You (aren't) ugly."

9.   **Eloise's March 7, 1863 Response to Ben**: Please see "Solution Number Eight" to read how to use Ben's family list code, as this is what Eloise used in her response to Ben. Using that list, she was able to respond: "Don't know information. Yes love." Then, later in the letter she explains that she is in Baselton, Pennsylvnia. In this paragraph, she hides the phrase, "No(t) truth," in the hope that he will understand that this is not her true location. While not particularly elaborate, she knows that as this is not a typically encrypted message, anyone, like John, looking over the message before it is sent should hopefully not be able to pick up on any treachery. Additionally, she needed something she could write very quickly and under a watchful eye.

10.   **Ben's April 11, 1863 Letter to Eloise**: The numbers, which were accurately deciphered not only by Eloise, but by the Confederates, indicate a modified Polybius square. This method uses a 5x5 grid with each letter corresponding to a horizontal and then vertical number. Thus, typically, A would be 11, B would be 12, and so on and so forth. Ben reminds her of "ij" because the I and J share the same square to account for the extra twenty-sixth letter in the English alphabet. Having the I and J share the same square is a very common method. However, Ben also uses a code word, which he underlines in his letter: love. Therefore, the L goes in the A location, O in B, V in C, and E in D.

The letters L, O, V, and E are skipped when it comes time to insert them in the alphabet, creating a grid that looks like this:

	1	2	3	4	5
1	L	O	V	E	A
2	B	C	D	F	G
3	H	I/J	K	M	N
4	P	Q	R	S	T
5	U	W	X	Y	Z

Using the above grid, you can assume that each pair of numbers stands in for one letter. To make it visually overwhelming, Ben did not separate the pairs of letters, but you can do this yourself, making the initial number-combinations 1-1, 1-4, 1-5, and 1-3, or L, E, A, V. Continuing in this manner creates the following message: leave baselton its too close to darby where we moved confederate weapons and supplies.

But that's not all! If you only found the first code in this letter, you may wish to stop reading, as there are *two* codes hidden in this letter.

Ben specifically made the first code long and complicated with all of the numbers. However, his hope was that he would capture the attention of whomever would most assuredly read it before Eloise, thus distracting him or her from his real message while also putting false information into the Confederate army's hands. By simply using the first letter of every one of his sentences, you get the following message: let them have that period know location yet question I love you

As punctuation would look wildly out of place at the beginning of a sentence, he attempted to rectify the problem by adding in "period" and "question" to show the difference between these sentences.

Therefore, Ben's true message to Eloise was actually

instructing her to let them have the first message. This would help build her credibility, as she could provide them with a decoded message that another expert within the Confederate army might confirm. This would also hopefully tell Eloise that she was not giving the Confederates proprietary information by decoding the numbers. Additionally, Ben showed his true hand to Eloise, asking if she had any information yet on the location of the weapons and supplies, having lied in the numbers by pretending to already have those items. Finally, the "I Love You" was simply for her to know and hold onto.

11. **Eloise's Letter to Ben While Traveling:** This letter does two things. It contains an expected secret to show John, but it also contains the true message to Ben. The easiest to see and solve would be the picture code on the bottom. Starting at the dot, Ben would simply have to use an equal unit's worth of space in the directions written by Eloise to draw a picture. The finished picture would be a heart at the bottom of the letter. The message in the letter itself is hidden a bit better, in order to avoid detection by John. At the beginning of the letter, she emphasizes times, mentioning the "five" and the "middle." This is Eloise's way of letting Ben know that he should pull out the middle letter of all five-letter words. For example, her first five-letter word, "after," would give you a "t." This is eventually followed by the five-letter word "reuse," giving you a "u." Pulling out the middle letter of every five-letter word spells out the following message: TURNERSVILLE HEADED TO DARBY WITH ONE HUNDRED MEN. This finally gives Ben the location he needed, Turnersville, while also warning him about the intended destination and number of those coming to retrieve the weapons and supplies.

12. **Ben's Threatening Letter:** Yes, this is a rather lengthy threat to Eloise's supposed kidnappers. However, Ben also uses it to send a rather simple message to Eloise, assuming she would have the opportunity to read it as he knows she has not actually been kidnapped. By underlining the phrase "beginning of the

end," he's sending the key to Eloise. Simply, you have to read the beginnings of the ends. In other words, collect all of the first letters of the last words in the sentences. (The first sentence is not included, as it is the key to the cipher.) This should spell out the following message: SEE YOU IN TURNERSVILLE. He clearly got Eloise's message about the true location of the supplies, and is on his way.

13. **The Soldiers in Miston**: Given that Eloise is fully aware that Ben knows she hasn't been kidnapped, she has to assume the soldiers in Miston who are supposedly looking for her are in on the secret with Ben and have been sent for some purpose. In their discussion, they clearly try to get some alone time with her, though Eloise sees, based on John's reaction, that that could be dangerous. Therefore, she tries to assure Ben that she is still all right, especially as he may be worried following the events in Darby wherein she could have potentially lost value in John's eyes. She therefore tries to send a message to Ben that, yes, she is safe. She attempts to do this by swearing on her Aunt Bessie's grave in New York. She quickly uses the same "either/or" message system using Ben's false family members that she used before. (See Solution Eight for the full list and explanation.) Aunt Bessie in New York translates to "yes," meaning that yes, she *is* safe. Also, note that as the Aunt Bessie example is number two, the word "safe" is the second word after the introduction of Aunt Bessie in New York. Then, when the soldiers ask if they would like to be staying in the inn that night, Eloise quickly references her other Aunt Bessie from New Jersey, which means "no." Here, again, the word inn is the second word after the introduction of the Aunt Bessie from New Jersey. However, if the soldiers did not pick up on that more minor detail, Ben could probably still assume what the "yes" and "no" are in reference to as they're fairly direct answers to the topics introduced by the soldiers.

To fully explain Eloise's "no" in response to staying at the inn, Eloise truly loves Ben. Therefore, she would hardly like to find herself in an inn that night with John, unsure of his intentions. But then the soldiers leave suddenly after her initial "no" response in the alley, causing her to wonder how much they really know. However, it is assumed that the soldiers needed to repeat her words back to Ben, who is nearby. For later they come into the inn with a message meant to dissuade John and Eloise from spending the night there. Therefore, one can assume that her "no" response was properly deciphered and dealt with before things could become awkward or even dangerous for her.

14. **Eloise's Message from the Burning Farmhouse**: Eloise realized, even in the chaos of the fire and battle, that if she were to make it out of the farm alive with Ben, she may have some explaining to do depending on who were to find them together. She hoped she would still have some clout with the Confederate soldiers, but she would need a way to explain her presence with Ben. So, this message was written as a sort of secondary form of protection since she didn't know who she might come across outside of the farmhouse. Therefore, she hastily scribbled this note. The R   2 means to move over that number of spaces within the alphabet, using a simple Caesar cipher. (She certainly didn't have time for any code fancier than that, and she also wanted to make sure that any potential questioners would feel confident enough to try to solve it, putting the bulk of their attention on this note rather than herself or Ben.) So, in a situation where 1=A, 2=B, 3=C, and 4=D, you would have to move two letters to the right. So, instead 1=C, 2=D, 3=E, and 4=F. Similarly, you can assume that 25=A and 26=B, if you were to loop the alphabet around on itself in order to complete the pattern of moving two to the right. Therefore, her message reads: THE PURPOSE OF THIS MESSAGE IS TO SIMPLY BUY ME TIME

15. **Ben's Final Message to Eloise**: Under the willow tree near their homes, Ben gives Eloise a message that he would like her to read before they see their families after about a year away

from them. Ben's instructions are to "simply continue without lifting from the paper unless directed to do so by the dotted line." He also writes that the message is comprised of four words. Following that are four rows. Each row is a word. The lines and symbols are all strokes of the pen. And the numbers above each initial stroke indicate how many strokes are involved in each letter. So, for example, the first word has four letters in it. We know this because it labels the strokes associated with each letter: 4, 3, 2, and 2. After this, you alternate until you run out of strokes. Additionally, arrows indicate in which direction your stroke should start. So, for the first word, the downward stroke is the first of four strokes for that letter. The second stroke is the first stroke of the second letter, and so on and so forth. The first word is "WILL." Each stroke is combined by alternating in order until the strokes are completed. The first word has strokes going in this order: W, I, L, L, W, I, L, L, W, I, W. The second and third stroke for the letter I are shown in relation to an existing stroke, the first, as you must lift your pen between strokes. If no pen lift is indicated, follow Ben's instructions to "continue without lifting from the paper." The next word is YOU: Y, O, U, Y, Y. The third word is MARRY: M, A, R, R, Y, M, A, R, R, Y, M, A, R, R, Y, M. And the fourth word is ME: M, E, M, E, M, E, M, E. This results in the question "WILL YOU MARRY ME" to which we can assume Eloise's answer is a confident and joyous "yes."

ABOUT THE AUTHOR

Ellen Parry Lewis

Ellen Parry Lewis is the author of seven other novels and one nonfiction book. She is also the editor of two short story collections. This is her first interactive book. Elllen lives in New Jersey with her husband, daughter, son, and super fluffy golden Labrador.

BOOKS BY THIS AUTHOR

Future Vision

Samantha Bell is an ambitious high school student with a bright future until one fateful night at the local fair. She decides to go through the controversial Future Vision exhibit. This attraction allows viewers to see up to twenty seconds of their personal future. Because of the possible risks, viewers must ingest a dissolvable pill immediately afterward, causing them to forget what they had just witnessed. Samantha tries to take the future into her own hands, though, when she smuggles a pen inside the attraction. Although she was forced to forget what she had seen, she leaves the attraction with an ominous feeling and three mysterious words written on her hand: Snow, fight, and ca. Samantha feels she must figure out what those three words mean before the event occurs and possibly ruins her life.

Avenging Her Father

A strange twist of fate allows the lovely Laersona Wylos to narrowly escape death in the ethnic cleansing of the Peretians ordered by the cruel King Laurenso. Her father was not as fortunate and was brutally murdered by the king's men. Heartbroken and alone, Laersona vows to avenge him and her people by destroying the man who ordered their demise. Her thirst for royal blood takes her on a dangerous journey to the castle where she meets the king's dashing young prince and learns shocking royal secrets. Will her growing feelings for the prince distract her from her true purpose and how will he react when he discovers her quest for revenge?

An Unremarkable Girl

Krisanna Wether happily lived in a peaceful farming village until it was raided and her people were enslaved by a neighboring kingdom. She finds herself in a dangerous situation where she is mistaken for a traveling princess. While living under this false identity, Krisanna meets a handsome, kind enemy soldier who makes her question her hatred towards her captors. Her feelings toward him blossom, enveloping him in her dangerous web of deceit.

Krisanna's efforts to free her family and people take this once seemingly unremarkable farm girl on a journey as a prisoner, a princess, a fugitive, a foreigner, a member of nobility, and more. She soon discovers that in order to save her people and the man she has grown to love, she will have to make difficult decisions that challenge her definitions of good and evil.

Risking A Life

Constantly surrounded by luxury, but unable to partake in it, eighteen-year-old maid Louisa West is unsatisfied with her life. On New Year's Eve 1854, though, she gains knowledge that will change her life forever. A man tells her of a demon in the woods—a demon who offers wagers resulting in either unfathomable fortune or irreversible loss. If the person wins, they gain a promised reward. If they lose, the cost is the life of another person. Finding that she can no longer take her current circumstances, Louisa desperately seeks out the mysterious demon. She gambles the life of a fellow servant to find romance with the dashing and wealthy William Knight. As time unfolds, Louisa realizes that she has made a terrible mistake—one that could lead to death and lost love.

Blood Moon

Sarah and her mother are Hersotes, people immortal and capable of magic. However, on a trip to an island as a young child, Sarah uses magic found in a Blood Moon to accidentally kill her mother who she thought could never die. Years later, Sarah learns of another impending Blood Moon, and the fears she has pushed aside resurface as she wonders what damage she might do this time. With the company of her close friends, Sarah journeys to that horrible island from her past in an attempt to discover the Blood Moon's dark secrets—secrets that could result in the deaths of not just one unfortunate person, but thousands. And Sarah may be the only key to changing these people's fate

Crowning Achievement

Julie Pike is out of her league—way out. She is more comfortable in ice hockey gear than high heels, but when her high school guidance counselor suggests beefing up her resume with something outside of sports, Julie figures the Miss Lauring Township Scholarship Pageant is the least objectionable option. However, when strange things start to happen, contestants begin to drop out. It's clear that someone is trying to fix the outcome of the pageant—or worse, destroy it. As the numerous pranks escalate, Julie has to keep her eyes and ears open as she tries to figure out who is behind this and why. With the help of the extremely ambitious contestant, Lily, and her next-door neighbor, Mason, Julie begins to uncover secrets that have origins and consequences beyond the pageant spotlights.

Because She Fell Asleep

Ember Amato is the prototypical high school senior, with a busy schedule, great friends, and a caring boyfriend. But her life takes a surprisingly dark turn when her best friend, Janell, falls asleep on the school bus one morning, waking up at a ramshackle house in the woods. Though presumably telling Ember all about the strange conversation she overheard there, Janell's disappearance one night speaks of her having held some information back. In pursuit of her best friend, Ember discovers a brutal murder. Fearing that a police investigation has grown cold, Ember puts it upon herself to look into these horrifying occurrences, However, in so doing, she sets off an unpredictable and dangerous chain of events.

Smarty Pants: How To Become A Valedictorian

Being the valedictorian or salutatorian of your graduating class may open many doors, including valuable scholarships to attend college and coveted high profile internships to help get a step ahead of your classmates. Becoming a valedictorian is hard work, but just getting straight A's may not be enough. In Smarty-Pants: How to Become a Valedictorian, Ellen Parry Lewis shares her personal story, along with stories from other valedictorians on the specific strategies and actions they took to earn the honor of being chosen as valedictorian for their graduating class.

In this book you will learn

-Specific strategies to boost your GPA
-The importance of your social game
-How your teachers can help you
-How your competition can help you
-The one simple step you can take to improve your essays
-The importance of extra credit assignments
-The benefits...and dangers...of taking honors and AP classes
-How getting a 100% can actually HURT your GPA
-When skipping school can HELP your GPA
-How to find out how your school's GPA is calculated
-Who to pick as partners when given a special class assignment and why

-How to select the extracurricular activities that may help you get into the college you want
-How to have fun while doing the hard work necessary to graduate top of your class

This book is not for everyone. Some students are simply satisfied with graduating from high school. There can only be one valedictorian and one salutatorian for each graduating class. This book does not guarantee that you will be a valedictorian. Your results may vary and each school has different criteria for selecting these top spots.

If becoming valedictorian or salutatorian is important to you, read this book. But be warned: Don't recommend it to your classmates who are graduating the same year you are....You don't want them to know what you know.

If you know someone who wants to become a valedictorian or salutatorian, or someone who wants to improve their GPA, give them this book.

Night Light: Haunted Tales Of Terror

Night Light: Haunted Tales of Terror will keep you up at night with tales of creatures from deep underground coal mines in the the Appalachian Mountains, ghostly apparitions, mysterious prayer circles, a pact with the devil and blood curdling screams of the Jersey Devil haunting a couple in the middle of the night in the New Jersey Pine Barrens. Featuring new suspense and horror stories from Mid-Atlantic authors Ellen Parry Lewis, SF Varney, Charles Matthew, Virginia Parrish and Sammi Caramela.

"May All My Dreams Come True" by Ellen Parry Lewis

Bridget Brown's life certainly isn't the worst thing it could be; she has a house, a steady job, a close group of friends. And yet with the excitement of her friends' lives greatly overshadowing her own existence, she finds herself making a fateful wish on her birthday. "May all my dreams come true." However, she might not be prepared for what that means.

"Forgetting to Remember" by Sammi Caramela

Dahlia's nerves are already shot to pieces. But when she sees an ex-boyfriend near her home in Philadelphia, she finds that her life can get even more complicated.

"The Gig" by Charles Matthews

At only twenty-three years old, Julian Todenby is already at the top of his game, working in huge company's marketing department. However, after winning a trip to Canada through his company, he begins seeing an unsettling little boy. He very quickly starts to worry that this trip is not the prize he had hoped for and that true terror might be just around the corner.

"Prayers in the Dirt" by Ellen Parry Lewis

Naomi is new to her South Jersey neighborhood. At first, she loves the woods behind her house, and is enjoying a walk there when she spots something in the dirt--a prayer sketched in the soft earth. She quickly finds that that's not the only thing in those woods.

"I Know You are Awake" by SF Varney

The Crug. It is unknown by many, including ten-year-old Johnny. But some in the Appalachian Mountains say that this creature, reeking of sulfur, came straight from Hell. Imaginative Johnny knows fact from fiction, though, and assumes that this is just a scary story. But the dark winter night may hold more than just stories.

"Mom and Me" by Sammi Caramela

Cassie and her mom are close. Very close. And so when Cassie's mom doesn't come home when she's supposed to, she immediately knows that something is wrong. And she very quickly realizes that it has something to do with the man nearby her house, watching her.

"It's Not the House" by Virginia Parrish

Jack and Robin have renovated homes before. Why should the old house in the New Jersey Pine Barrens be any different? Who cares if the house had once belonged to some family named Leeds? And yet, after hearing some howling in the woods, Robin begins to hint to Jack that perhaps they should care about the house's history.

Horror On Holiday: 13 Tales Of Terror

Horror on Holiday: 13 Tales of Terror is a bakers dozen of illustrated chilling stories from the mind of Jolene Wightman. Each story is set during a different holiday proving once and for all that horror is a year round affair. Featuring spooky and ethereal illustrations by SF Varney. Filled with stories of aliens, frightful creatures, witches and ghostly apparitions, this book is perfect for reading by flashlight under the covers. Read if you dare!

ACKNOWLEDGEMENTS

Every time I sit down to write, I start by praying. I thank God for the ability to write, and that I choose the best words and story to tell. God has blessed me beyond measure, and I'm so thankful for the opportunities I've received while following my passion.

Sam, thank you for your continued support through Metal Lunchbox Publishing. I can't believe how many books and years have passed, and I'm truly thankful for all you've done for me.

Al, I finally listened and wrote about your suggested subject. You have always supported me as I follow my dreams, and I am forever grateful to have you as my partner through life.

I'm so thankful for my first readers --- my parents. Mom and Dad, thanks for reading my book, offering me feedback, and working diligently on all of the codes! You two have always been there for me. I am blessed beyond measure to have been raised by such incredible people.

While I enjoyed creating the codes in this book, I couldn't have done one in particular without help from Virginia Parrish, who is an incredibly gifted author herself. Thank you!

Also, thank you to Jayden Dalglish for lending me your artistic skills and helping me with the picture code. I can't wait to read your future books because you are honestly one of the most talented authors I've ever read.

And last, but certainly not least, thank you to my kids, Estellise and Gavin. You two inspire me every day. You cheer me on, ask about my work, and I'm so blessed to be your mom.